A
Muse
Meant

Phyl Campbell

Also by Phyl Campbell

For Teens and Adults

Mother Confessor One

Mother Confessor Two

The Carley Patrol

#25 Reasons
Why Charlie Should Never
Read Jane's Books to Jane

For Children of all Ages

Martha's Chickens and the Pirates

I'm Not Writing a Book Today

Nonfiction

Confessions of a Grammar Enthusiast

A

Muse

Meant

Phyl Campbell

A Muse Meant

Copyright © 2016 by Phyl Campbell

A Muse Meant / Phyl Campbell

ISBN 13: 978-1484029886

ISBN-10: 1484029887

Printed in the United States of America

Young Adult Fantasy Fiction: Best friends experience growing pain; Samm finds magic house in an abandoned high school and accidentally lets Goons escape.
1.Young Adult: Fantasy Fiction

To Samantha and her parents,
Alejandro and Veronica.
Your journey has been amazing;
you've certainly inspired me.

And

To Sean and Josh: for believing I
can do impossible things –
and letting me.

The Lame Field Trip

"It might not be THAT bad. Somebody did science magic for the talent show last year, remember? It was pretty cool. This trip could be like that."

Still arguing, best friends Alex and Samm dismounted their bikes and entered Alex's white stucco house.

"That was a two-minute act. This is a full day science program put on by the drama department." Alejandro Cervantes, called Alex, complained as he handed his mother his permission slip and then slid into his usual place at the kitchen table. "How magical could it be?"

Alex's mother accepted the permission slip, but otherwise stayed out of the conversation. She knew his friend could handle him. She did raise her eyebrow reading that the field trip was tomorrow – meaning her son had probably lost more than one copy of the form before this one made it to her hands.

"It's not just magic, though," Samantha Cisneros, better known as Samm, added as she set down her backpack and took her usual place at the table of the Cervantes home. Unlike many other Hispanic families, Alex and Samm were both only children, one of many reasons they appeared glued at the hip. "It's a science center. There are supposed to be live demonstrations and a climbing wall and a construction lab. There's even a food kitchen and a menagerie."

"Coffee filter butterflies and stuffed animals do not make a menagerie." Alex retorted.

"STUFFED animals? Are you serious?"

"No joke." Alex assured. "They have a real tent set up, but the campfire is fake with red and orange tissue paper taped to real logs. Then they have a big woven basket with stuffed animals and puppets. My coach let us use his account to see their Facebook page. I saw pictures. Not cool."

"They have a Facebook page?"

"Everybody has a Facebook page. Except us."

Samm didn't say anything.

Alex looked up.

"You got a Facebook page?" It was more accusation than question.

"I didn't want to tell you." Samm replied meekly.

"When did you get a Facebook page?"

"When I turned thirteen last month." Samm blurted. "I was going to wait, but"

"But you got one! And you didn't tell me!"

"I didn't want you to think I was rubbing it in." Samm continued to speak in a rush, trying to simultaneously justify her actions and not hurt her best friend. "You'll be thirteen in a few months and then we'll both have one. Mrs. Darling wasn't busy one day and she knows Mama's scared of social media stuff, and she asked me if I wanted help with it, so I went ahead. But it's boring without you on it, too."

"It's not the same." Alex's tone was deflated.

"I don't even use mine! It's just set up and waiting, OK?!"

"I still can't believe you didn't tell me!"

"I'm really sorry, Alex."

Alex huffed and didn't reply.

"Don't stay mad at me. Tell me what you saw from the coach's page. Or, can we go online now and you can show me? You can see that I haven't done anything with my page. It's really no big deal."

Mrs. Cervantes gave them permission and Alex pulled up the site.

"They don't even have a webpage?"

"Nope. Already checked. Just this."

It did look disappointing, to say the least. If they were seven, instead of seventh graders, it might have looked a little better than a pediatrician's waiting room. There was a rock climbing wall, but it was no grander than the one they had in their elementary school gym. There was a campsite with a real tent set up, but Alex was right. The animals were stuffed and the campfire was tissue and construction paper. There were some kiddie folding tables with rocks and some display boards with pictures and paragraphs of type to read. It looked less impressive than a science fair where the kids did all the projects themselves.

"We could make the best of it," Samm said optimistically. "Where are the kitchen experiments?"

"I don't see any kitchen pictures," Alex replied.

"Do you think that's bad?"

Alex scoffed. "I don't think it's good."

"The permission slip says we're going to watch a planetarium show."

"Betcha it's on VHS."

Alex chuckled, and Samm did, too, for a minute. Then she sighed.

"Well, it's still a field trip, which means no class and no homework tomorrow."

"True." Alex tried to think of something positive to say. Why was he always Mr. Negativity lately? "And maybe I'll make my own kitchen experiment and get food poisoning so I won't have to go."

"Alex!" Samm chided. "We'll have a good time, regardless. We'll be together." Samm nodded her head, eager to end that topic of conversation.

"Speaking of a good time," — Alex was as relieved as Samm was for their fight to be over — "What time is your game on Saturday?"

"One? I think? Let me check the calendar at home and call you tonight."

"Yes, please. Not that I want to go or anything. You know, if I have nothing better to do."

Mrs. Cervantes made a disgruntled noise.

Samm laughed, but then realized that Alex wasn't laughing. But of course he was joking. He went to so many of her games, her coach called Alex the honorary mascot.

While she was trying to puzzle that out, the phone rang in the living room. Mrs. Cervantes went to answer it.

"Five bucks says it's your mother." Alex grinned.

"I bet you're right. But it's not too late. I wonder why she's calling."

"Samm," Mrs. Cervantes re-entered the kitchen. "Your mom says it's time for soccer practice. She's coming to get you, so you better be ready."

"Oh, shoot! I forgot about practice tonight!" Samm yelped. Then she remembered her manners. "Yes, ma'am." She got up to leave. "See you tomorrow?"

"Unless I have food poisoning. Call me when you get home from practice."

"Will do."

Saturday's game was the regional soccer championship match. Samm's team had beat out thirteen other girls' teams to earn a coveted spot. In the past, Alex and Samm had played on the same co-ed team. They had met as soccer players on the preschool field. But at the middle school level, boys and girls were separated. The better soccer players on the boy's teams switched over to playing football, so Alex's team fought hard but didn't even make it to the semis.

Samm didn't make it past Alex's front step. Her mother's van was in the driveway.

"Your bag's in the back already, *mija*. Your dinner's in the front seat."

"Mom, what time is the game Saturday? I was going to tell"

"Alex. Always Alex. Alejandro can wait until tomorrow. You were at his house so long I had to come get you."

"If I had a cell phone, you could text me."

"Don't be silly. You don't need one of those. You're only thirteen. You go to school, to practice, and home."

"But Mama."

"No, but Mama. Papi works very hard to provide for our family. I work hard to take care of our home. You work hard at school and at soccer. But you won't ask your father for something so expensive as a phone. We grew up without one and you will, too."

Samm knew it was pointless to argue with her mother at that point. She thought again how lucky Alex was that his mom had a job. She understood things like texting and Facebook and being connected online. Samm and the librarian set up her Facebook account at school because Samm could only get on the home computer when her father was home. By then, it was time for dinner and then unwinding, as he called it, in front of the television.

***

Practice ran longer than expected, and it was too late to call Alex when Samm got home. She was exhausted anyway. She would try to remember to tell him in the morning.

Future-Shroom and Fear

Samm could not tear herself away from the conversation she was hearing. She was listening in on a conversation she was apparently having with Alex, but both of them were vaguely older. Alex was delivering some devastating news.

"I don't want to stop you from living your life. I mean, there's nothing wrong with you."

"But I just can't let you."

"Look, my dad talks about leaving all the time. We might leave before it happens."

"Leave? You can't leave!"

"And then there'd be nothing to worry about."

"Nothing to worry about? Are you crazy?"

"Because I'd be gone see – and you'd move on."

"How can you even say that? You're my best friend!"

"And you're mine. And I will never forget you. Not as long as I live."

A MUSE MEANT

Samantha took the headphones off her ears and wiped her eye on her shirtsleeve. She didn't get off the double capped mushroom marked "Future-shroom." She didn't venture over to the funhouse mirrors of the mushroom next to her – though she was tempted. She continued to sit cross legged on the lazily revolving pedestal of the mushroom while her head went mad trying to identify plausible explanations and justify the irrational tears rolling down her face. She wouldn't have gotten off at all, but the roller coaster came to a stop beside her.

This roller coaster lacked wheeled cars; instead, huge boa constrictors — each longer than Samm was tall — bit each other's tails in an endless serpentine ribbon. On the backs of the serpents were rows of something between saddles and carnival seats. Samm had no idea how they were attached to the snakes or if they were held there by centripetal motion. The three story drop had riders screaming at regular intervals. A clear glass tube kept the bottom half of the snakes contained in the ride.

However, while Samm stood there staring, the boa nearest her popped its head off the tail it had been biting and hissed in her face, scaring her off the toadstool. She did not turn around to see if it left the ride completely to follow her.

She entered the ice cream parlor and all but forgot about the boa as soon as she did. This was a happy place, almost like a 1950s American Diner, complete with Elvis tunes blaring from an old jukebox in the corner. Black and white checkered floors gave way to slim bar stools and a man in a white apron and cook's hat behind the counter. Sitting on the stools, she saw classmates in poodle skirts, white shirts, and rolled jeans and thought nothing unusual about it. Probably there were costumes behind the counter and you put them on over your clothes when you came in.

Samm waved to them, and they waved back. She was close enough she might have said something, but she was afraid to break the spell of the casual atmosphere. They were smiling at her, and not teasing her or ignoring her. She wasn't one to push her luck where her peers were concerned. She wasn't ready to put on a costume, and wasn't in the mood to eat ice cream either, but she stood at the edge of the room and just took in the scene.

16

A MUSE MEANT

The cool room helped steady her nerves and dry her tears. The conversation which caused her to shed them moments earlier was already ebbing from her consciousness.

Even so, Samantha missed Alex. And with the conversation she could almost remember, she worried if Alex was only subjected to some twenty-four-hour bug. He'd seemed fine yesterday, but when Samm stopped in front of his house so they could bike to school together, his mother had come out to tell her that he was sick and wouldn't be coming after all. Did she seem especially concerned about her sick son? Samm didn't think so, but she couldn't be sure.

Although she enjoyed being in the ice cream parlor, the man behind the counter's friendly face shifted a few times to impatient — clearly if Samm wanted to order, he would need to be ready with a cheerful smile and helpful attitude. But Samm wasn't ready. She was resolved to see more.

At first, she considered going back to the Futureshroom, but the roller coaster had not resumed its course and the boa glared at her menacingly. Who ever heard of a roller coaster guided by boa constrictors? She saw the sign marked "theater/menagerie" and decided to venture that way instead.

Samantha would have thought the theater and the menagerie would have been two separate locations. This was not the case. The stage was three large slowly revolving platforms being turned on the bottom level, as she would discover, by a menagerie of animals.

Samantha entered the stage on the top level. The revolving stage made her slightly seasick, but she fought off her queasiness as she approached the edge of the stage. The spotlights were too bright, and the few chaperones that had been stationed there were oblivious to the monkey maneuvers of her classmates.

Samantha edged out as she dared, but her classmates were giving no pause in their pursuit of each other over the wooden guard rail and down to the next level. Perhaps on the second level, she would feel more secure. Perhaps there would be a dramatic enterprise she could join in – Samantha loved acting. She found a sign marked "stairs" and followed it to a hole with the tip of a ladder sticking out the top.

"Great. More heights." She gripped the edges of the ladder. It was not connected to the stage, and wobbled precariously. "Terrific." She muttered.

She sat on the edge of the hole, and rocked the ladder back and forth. When she was satisfied that the ladder couldn't fall past the hole, she went ahead and placed her left foot on a rung. The ladder wobbled, and Samantha's arms were shaking, too. She thought very seriously about getting up and going back to the door, but she didn't know if she could get to the menagerie any other way, and she was already on her way if she could just muster the courage to place her other foot on the ladder. Again, she tilted the ladder to reassure herself that it couldn't fall. Then she placed her right foot on the ladder and straightened.

"Don't look down. Don't be a baby."

One foot at a time, she made her way down the ladder. She could see and hear her classmates all around, clambering over the front edges of the stage, and wondered why none of them were using the ladder. Just before she reached the rung she would use to move herself to the second stage, her foot slipped. Surprised, she lost her hold on the ladder and

19

slid down to the first stage, where she landed on her rump with one hand on a cow pie.

"Fantastic." She wiped her hand on the floor to remove as much manure as she could. She knew her hand would stink regardless, but she didn't want to brush it up against her clothes accidentally before she could find a bathroom to wash it off.

"Move it girly." A fat ugly man with terrible breath and body odor held a pitchfork in his hand. As Samm rolled quickly out of the way, the man used the pitchfork to stab the cowpie.

"You broke it, girly." He complained. "Bad girly. Go away."

Samm stood. She would not show this jerk that she was afraid. "I was just leaving." She said. She placed her clean hand on the handle of the door that suddenly appeared on her right. She pushed the door open, and, with more bravado than she felt, she said "what a clown!"

For Your Muse, Meant

Though Samm was positive she had entered the stage on the top floor, the other side of the door revealed that she was at the same door she had used to get to the top of the stage. She had been told the building was the former high school, and lots of gyms doubled as theater spaces, so finding a stage in the gym wasn't too surprising. Seeing animals in the abandoned gym was a little weird but it wasn't like students were playing basketball there anymore. Still, three levels of the stage should not meet in the same place on the other side. Samm wondered whether she would be on the top floor or the bottom if she went back through the door again.

But after hearing the conversation on the revolving mushroom and being frightened by the biting boa coaster, a multi-level stage with a single door was not the weirdest thing Samm had experienced on this field trip. So she went with it.

Nothing more than clowns at a carnival, she decided. She looked around and didn't see a bathroom; however, she spied a janitor's closet next to the ice cream parlor.

Thankfully, she found she could work the knobs. Even better, unlike most public school bathrooms, the hot water was actually hot, and the soap dispenser worked. Once her hand was clean, Samm felt better – almost normal. She left the janitor's closet feeling good enough to wonder -- if the man in the menagerie was a janitor as she suspected, why didn't he use the hot water to bathe once in a while? She giggled at the thought.

"If there is one thing I cannot abide, Madame, it is for persons to mock those less fortunate." The voice belonged to a stern old man. It was crisp and precise, and more than a little menacing. "Do not laugh at my Goons."

Samm did not immediately look up. She was scared and being nervous made it harder for her to stop laughing. She fought to get control over her face so he didn't have a reason to punish her – he was an adult, even if she didn't know him and he wasn't her teacher. Samm definitely feared authority. Still, she was curious. "Goons? The janitors?"

"My caretakers. They took care of me and now I take care of them. There is nothing funny about them and they certainly are not clowns. This park is for your muse meant, not your mundane sense of humor."

"For my amusement?"

"No – A Muse Meant is a play on words, Samantha. This place is for your muse, meant. It is a place meant for your muse – to be a place of objects to think and ponder upon."

Samm looked up at the speaker. He was not a tall man, but he was very slender and that made him appear taller than he was. He was wearing the vest, shirt, and pants of a working man's suit – formal yet allowing for feats of strength to be performed, not unlike the lion tamer or strongman at the circus. Samm was thinking he reminded her of Count Olaf mixed with Professor Dumbledore and she couldn't decide whether she thought this man was mysteriously good or inherently evil. He wasn't much taller than she was. He had thick white hair that formed a partial wreath around his head. Similar fluffy white hair formed a goatee around his mouth and chin. If Samm focused on the fluffiness of his hair, he did not look menacing. But when her eyes met his, she was terrified.

"Perhaps you would rather join your friends in the Present?" He gestured to the ice cream parlor where several students were sitting on stools enjoying frozen desserts. He frowned. "Though perhaps it's not YOUR present, is it? But trifles, trifles." He waved his hand in a gesture of swatting carelessly at a fly, showing that he felt the time period was of little importance.

Seeing as he appeared to have stepped out of history, Samm wasn't surprised by his cavalier attitude.

"Anyway, it's not too late to be one of them, Samantha. Leave the future until it's the present, my dear. Worrying about it won't change it. Living is the only cure – and everybody dies from that."

"Everybody dies? So he is going to die? Is that -"

"The boas work together to ensure a smooth, yet exhilarating ride," declared the man to a group of spectators who magically appeared. The group was odd, since Samm thought the center was closed to anyone not in her class. Perhaps she'd misunderstood. They were back in front of the boa coaster — as Samm could now read on the sign on the arch over her head where the crowd was gathered – even though Samm was certain she hadn't taken a step away from the ice cream parlor. But now it was across the room, and she had to turn around to see it. "As they bite each other's tails, their serpentine coils quiver and shake, giving a unique experience each ride – not like those silly contraptions with tracks and wheels."

Samm had never heard of anyone scoffing at roller coasters before. Be afraid of them – certainly. Samantha was herself appropriately weary of impending death from falls of great distance. But to scoff at their simplicity? That was a new one for her.

"Oh, I suppose mundane roller coasters have their place." Samantha knew he was looking right at her now. She didn't know whether to be embarrassed or proud that they were on the same wavelength. "But of course I prefer these mighty beasts."

The host reached down to pat the nearest boa's head. It popped its head off the tail it was biting and hissed at him menacingly. He chuckled in response. "Oh, not to worry," he addressed the children, "they are prone to biting, but I haven't lost a person yet. Not even a digit." And he chuckled again. The boa went back to biting the tail in front of it. The coaster resumed its movement around the track. And Samm realized that was weird because people had not stopped screaming during the drop. No one got on or off the ride. But people screamed as they dropped.

Samantha heard the man chuckle again. She would not call it a pleasant chuckle. In fact, it made her spine feel like ice was tickling up it. A part of her liked it – the part that liked to read a good mystery or wait to ambush someone while Trick-or-Treating. But the rest of her — the rest that wouldn't even dare to step foot inside a fake haunted house on Halloween, or ride on one of those roller coasters that her host scoffed at — didn't.

"Who are you?" Samm asked, more boldly than she felt.

"I am Mr. Rios." The man said.

"You're mysterious, all right," Samm agreed.

A MUSE MEANT

"As are you, my dear Samantha." Mr. Rios said thoughtfully. "Of all the guests enjoying my exhibits, you are the only one who has seen me – and all that A Muse Meant has to offer."

"I'm the only one?" Samm looked around, but the crowd who had raptly listened to Mr. Rios's explanation of the boa coaster seemed to melt into the background. There, but muted. They became like part of the scenery.

"No doubt young Alejandro would have been able to see it, too, with your help. Nevertheless, I shall be keeping an eye on you."

"You know about Alex? What do you mean, keeping an eye on me?"

"I really must be going. Good day, madame." Mr. Rios turned on his heel and walked away at a brisk clip that seemed to defy his advanced age.

Samm started to follow him, but tripped over a mop wielded by yet another burly janitor. Samm saw Mr. Rios disappear through a wide set of double doors as she turned to see what had tripped her. She was eye level with the janitor's butt crack; the sight was less than pleasant.

"Hey!" she said.

The janitor grunted, and swung his mop bucket fully into Samm, knocking her over. Samm smelled an eye watering stench of bad breath and body odor as the janitor hulked over her. "Bad girly."

Samm had the thought that the janitor wasn't exactly human. He was huge. He was ugly. He stank. And the guttural way with which he spoke those two simple words put her on edge.

"Go, bad girly. Go!"

Samm didn't hesitate. She turned and ran. This time, she found the doors outside and did not stop running until she was back on the bus. By the time she had calmed down, the class was exiting the building and coming toward her. In the front, a group of popular girls were talking and laughing with their arms linked. They looked so young – so carefree. They clearly had not had the same experience as Samm had. She took deep breaths and hoped her face didn't look too splotchy.

"Did you even get off the bus, Samm?" One of the girls asked.

Samm couldn't tell whether the question was meant to be rude or simply curious. "Yeah. Didn't you see me? I was with you most of the time." Sam didn't feel the need to mention her fringe position to the group, or why she left it. The girls didn't seem to notice.

"Whatever. Hey – where's Alex?"

"He's sick today."

"Oh – too bad. He's always good for a laugh."

"Do you remember that time…"

The girls moved to the back of the bus, recounting tales of Alex the comedian. Alex really didn't try to be funny, Samm thought. He did make a lot of keen observations. He made her laugh, but Samm wasn't sure he always meant to. Why did the girls make a point of asking about Alex? Didn't they realize he was gone before the trip? Samm's mind raced with possibilities. The girls weren't mean, necessarily, but normally left her and Alex alone. Samm preferred it that way. A lot of boys were starting to get silly about girls, making rude jokes or claiming the girls had cooties and couldn't be touched or something. She hoped her friendship with Alex would survive their upcoming teenage years.

Samm stared out the window, watching the houses and streets and ballfields and everything else pass by. She did not have a forte for directions, preferring a detailed map she could follow, a book she could read, or just to let her imagination wander as the world passed by. The crowded bus felt safe. The clamoring students didn't have a care in the world. Must be nice.

Samm had always had the weight of the world on her shoulders. There was so much she wanted to see and do and prove. Her parents had risked a lot moving to the United States so she could have a better life. The last thing she would ever want would be to disappoint them.

They got back to school at the end of the day and Samm rode her bike home alone. Her mind churned with the little she knew and so much she didn't know. She called Alex's house, but he was sleeping. She ate dinner with her family, helped with the dishes, and returned to her room. She tried to read her favorite book, *Sahara Special*, but couldn't concentrate. What made Samm special? What brilliant teacher would be able to unlock her special gifts?

Mr. Rios flashed in her mind then. What kind of man was he? Surely he was some kind of magician. But was he the good kind — or the bad?

Lies and Omissions

Samm was still thinking about everything she had seen and heard on the field trip when Alex arrived on his bike Friday morning. He didn't look like he had been sick, which Samm registered, but she was still seeing the other Alex in her mind's eye.

"Hey," Alex greeted.

"Because I'd be gone, see? And you'd move on." Samm recalled, straining to remember every word that Alex said to her on the Future-shroom.

"Hey!" Alex did not like being ignored. "Earth to Samm!"

"What?" Samm snapped back to the present. She knew that face. But she hadn't been ignoring him. Quite the opposite. But he didn't know that. "Oh, sorry. You ready to go?"

"Yeah – where were you?"

"I was right here, waiting for you," Samm said, pretending to misunderstand him because she wasn't ready to explain it to him yet. Alex would think she was crazy. Maybe even she thought she was crazy.

Alex frowned. "I know you're here, here. I know I'm in your driveway. But you were looking a million miles away. So where'd you go?"

"Are you feeling better?" She asked, deflecting his question with her own.

"Yeah. I just hated to miss the field trip." But then Alex grinned, and Samm knew he hadn't been sick at all.

"Right."

"Mom didn't believe me either. Wouldn't let me watch TV or anything. Made me stay in bed the whole day as punishment."

Alex may not have been sick, but Samm's stomach was churning. She swallowed hard. "But she let you stay home."

"Yeah. She said 'don't you ruin Samm's field trip, *mijo*.' And she told me if I couldn't be nice, then maybe I should just stay home. So I did."

"So you left me and you weren't even sick?!"

"I wasn't leaving YOU. Just the dumb trip."

"That's pretty low Alex. I can't believe your mom allowed that."

33

"Me, neither." Alex was grinning, but then saw the look on Samm's face and stopped.

"Well, at least you won't have make up work – because of the lame field trip and all." Samm practically spit the words out at him.

"Right. Right. So, how was it? Was I right? Was the science program as lame as I told you?"

All of a sudden, Samm couldn't tell Alex what she had heard and seen. It just didn't feel right.

"Samm? Was it lame?"

"Yes. It was lame of you to fake being sick and make me go all by myself."

"I meant the science trip."

Samm debated with herself how best to answer. "It was not right without you," she finally said. That was a safe answer that could be taken in a lot of different ways.

Alex saw through that immediately. "Now that's a non-answer if I ever heard one. Why are you being so weird, Samm? What gives?

"I think you still owe me for making me have to go all by myself," Samm challenged.

"What do you mean, all by yourself? You had the rest of our class with you, right? I just had my mom here at the house."

"Yeah, well, you know how it is. Either we're together or we're invisible? Anyway. It's done and you're not sick. Maybe someday you and I can go explore it again."

"You said it was lame. Why would you want to go back?"

"I didn't say it was lame. I said it wasn't the same without you." Samm faltered, not sure how much she wanted to reveal. "You do make everything more fun to be around."

"Well, there is that. I guess you'll have your secret then."

"What?" Samm protested.

"You're one of the WORST liars I know. Something happened. You don't want to tell me. Fine. I'm not mad. I'll just find out from somebody else."

"You do that, Alex." Samm wished she'd thought of that in the first place. They were almost at the front doors. What was Alex going to say when the other students told him about A Muse Meant?

35

"Race you!" She challenged instead.

"Hey!" Alex cried, struggling to get his feet pumping again. "I was very pretend sick yesterday, remember! Hey, wait up!"

The bike ride was uneventful – Samm thought it was odd that they could just ride to school casually with what she now knew. How could she go back to anything normal after yesterday's field trip? After A Muse Meant? And how would she protect Alex? Surely all their classmates would be talking about it.

Alex and Samm parted ways at the first bell. Alex had Pre-Algebra and Samm had Science. Then Alex would go to Art while Samm had Choir. They had English, lunch, and Social Studies together. Then Alex had PE sixth period while Samm had Pre-Algebra. Alex was in band last period while Samm was Mrs. Darling's library helper.

In science class, Samm had a sub, so instead of even trying to watch another video of Bill Nye the Science Guy with everyone whispering around her, Samm tried to lose herself in her book. She read the same sentence a hundred and fifty times. All the while, she wondered how Alex was dealing with

36

everything he was hearing about the field trip. How would the students explain the difference between the images they had seen on Facebook and what they actually witnessed? In some ways, it would be easier to talk to Alex once he knew what she and the class had experienced.

But when she took the seat next to his in English, it was business as usual. Mrs. O'Malley didn't even have them write an essay about their trip or a thank you to Mr. Rios. Instead, she was starting a poetry unit. Normally, Samm would have loved this. But why was nothing being said about Thursday's trip?

No one talked about it at lunch.

No one said anything during Social Studies fifth period, even though Mr. Scott made his usual crack about transporting hooligans. Samm thought surely he would say something else about driving the bus that took them to A Muse Meant, but he was referring an incident on his morning route, apparently.

The whole day, school was quiet. Eerily uneventful — in Samantha's opinion. There was one solution. She would have to take Alex to A Muse Meant and show him herself.

Penalty Sick

Alex hung up the phone. Again, no answer. He looked at the clock: 10:07. Samm didn't call him like she'd promised. She'd never forgotten before. Maybe she was still mad at him for faking sick and skipping the field trip. Or how he'd been so mean about her getting a Facebook account.

He got on his bike. "Ma! I'm leaving now!"

His mother had said he could go to the game and he could ride his bike if he couldn't get hold of Samm's mother, the game had already started, or they weren't playing too far away. But in an area with many soccer fields, and no answer at Samm's, Alex decided that was really open to interpretation. His mother would understand that he needed to make up with his best friend. If she didn't, he'd face the music when he got home – when all was right between him and Samm again.

A MUSE MEANT

As he pedaled, his feet pounded out the rhythm: Find Samm. Find Samm. Find Samm.

There were no cars at the first two fields. Alex really didn't expect to find any. The championship game would most likely be played in the nice fields on the other side of town by the new high school building. They were newest. Champions deserved the best. Samm deserved the best.

Samm was older than he was. He knew that. Some days, he even accepted it. And his mom was more understanding than hers about computer stuff and technology. Probably, although Alex didn't know for sure, it was because his mother could read English better than Samm's did, so could glance over a computer screen and know if he was being bullied or getting into cyber-trouble. Samm still told her mom what her papers said or had her Papi sign them. Alex wished he could get away with that sometimes, but he knew Samm put extra pressure on herself to be good and follow the rules so she didn't have to explain any bad notes. Too much pressure, Alex thought.

Like many children of immigrants, he and Samm considered themselves just Americans. Their mothers talked to each other in Spanish sometimes, but Alex and Samm only knew a little of their parents' language. Even so, some classmates still thought they were ESL students because they had brown skin. Like the time he went up to the new girl to tell her he liked her. She'd complimented him on his English. He asked her where her grandparents were from. When she said, "Germany, she guessed," he told her she spoke really good English for a German kid, and stormed off. She didn't get that he was mad, and she giggled at his retreating figure. He did not think he was being funny.

But he must have crossed the line with Samm, he thought as he got on his bike. He was so mad at himself! Why did he have to go and upset the one person who understood what it was like to be them? Why did he wait until the last minute to find out when and where she was playing? He tried to tell himself he wasn't jealous, that it was just a boy-thing that he forgot. But he knew that wasn't entirely true.

Thunderclouds loomed overhead threateningly. But there was nothing he could do about it now.

A MUSE MEANT

He had thought he was calling early enough to get a ride from Samm's mother, but when there was no answer, he wasn't sure what to think. He only knew he'd messed up and needed to fix it. So he jumped on his bike to fix it. After the first half mile, he wondered why he hadn't asked his mom to drive him. Pride, he guessed. And to punish himself. Maybe if he showed how hard he tried to make it up to her, and he was all sweaty and miserable, Samm would take pity on him and forgive him. Be a man, he thought. But was that what Samm wanted from him? Didn't seem like her. Seemed like him. What he wanted. He wanted to be a man – even if he wasn't sure what that meant or how to do it. He pedaled harder. Don't think about yourself now. Concentrate. Find Samm. Find Samm. Find Samm. Find Samm. Each foot pushed down a word as he pedaled and hoped he would find the field where she was playing.

He had to show her he wasn't mad that his team wasn't playing the championship and hers was – even though he wasn't happy about it. He had to show her it was OK that she had Facebook and all the other good stuff she had that wasn't OK with him. It wasn't fair, but that was his problem for having a later

41

birthday, not hers. Why couldn't people use grades to set the rules? But Samm didn't make those rules. It wasn't her fault. Her team making the championship game wasn't the reason his team didn't – that's just what happened. He had to go to the game and prove he wasn't a big jerk. Even if he had to ride his bike all over town to find her.

Find Samm. Find Samm. Find Samm. Find Samm.

He passed the high school soccer fields and thought he saw Samm's mom's car. But as he got closer, he realized it wasn't the right one.

And then the clouds couldn't hold another drop, dumping their load all over Alex.

"Great! Just what I needed!"

Now Alex was too far from home to turn around. When he found Samm's game, he reasoned, her mother could give him a ride home. She usually even had the bike rack on so he wouldn't have to leave his bike behind.

Six soggy fields later, he thought he'd seen Samm's car twice, but nothing. He was soaked. Nothing else to do but bike back home again.

A MUSE MEANT

***

"Oh, Alex! How could you be so stupid?" Samm tut-tutted as she came into his bedroom with a bowl of hot soup Sunday afternoon. She stepped over a wadded up shirt and politely ignored the mountain of tissues on the nightstand.

Alex tried to sit up and groaned. "Thanks for coming. You didn't have to."

"Of course I did, silly." Samm said, setting herself carefully on the edge of Alex's bed with the bowl of soup – careful not to sit on him.

In turn, he struggled to an upright position. He took the bowl from Sam and nestled it in his lap. Samm suppressed a grin as Alex took in deep breaths of the fragrant steam.

"Smell good?" She teased.

"It's wonderful."

"I know. It's a good thing I just ate, or that soup might not have made it upstairs to you."

"Mama would make you a bowl, if you want."

"Oh, no. I'm just teasing you. I ate before I came over. Both our Moms work wonders in the kitchen."

"You're right about that." Alex picked up the spoon, considered it for a minute, then put it down and picked up the bowl. He slurped some soup, returned the bowl to his lap, and exhaled. "That's good stuff."

"I'm glad."

"So what happened with your game yesterday? Are you going to show me your trophy?"

"No trophy yet. I didn't get a chance to call you. Because of the weather, the coaches cancelled the game early and Mom decided I needed new jeans, so she took me to the mall."

"Ugh. Shopping."

"Tell me about it."

"I'm glad you're not one of those girls who would drag me out to the mall to hang out."

"Well, maybe the bookstore."

"Chocolate shop."

"Game store?"

"Electronics store."

"And the Food Court isn't terrible."

"True."

"Anyway, when I got home and called, you had already left and your Mom didn't know where you were."

Samm looked around the room. She noticed that the decor had changed a lot over the years since her first visits. Gone, for example, were the trucks and trains that used to cover nearly every inch of space. The walls, formerly wallpapered with "Things That Go," were painted a fresh hunter green. De-motivational posters replaced instructions from made-up games and art projects dating all the way back to Kindergarten. The posters and paint were funded by Alex's elementary graduation gift from his abuela. He was so happy to be able to pick them out. Samm thought about the week they spent painting. It was a disaster and Alex's parents must have hired professionals to fix all their blunders. It looked great now. The Einstein calendar next to his desk was still on February. Samm itched to change that – it was nearly May. Alex's backpack spilled out onto his desktop, alongside various silver and black bits that looked like they might be pieces of some electronic gadget.

"I wasn't going to miss your game," Alex said, breaking Samm's train of thought. Samm was glad for the distraction.

Grinning at him, she retorted, "You'll be all better when we do play. The game's been rescheduled — two Saturdays from now."

"I'll try to be there." Alex grinned, then winced.

"Hurt bad?" Samm asked.

"Let's just say the next time I decide to bike all over town in the rain – I hope you are there to remind me how stupid an idea it is."

"Well, yeah. Why did you even do that?"

"In my defense, it wasn't raining when I left the house."

"Yeah?"

"And then when it started, I thought if I found your game, I could get a ride home from your mom."

"Well, yeah. That makes sense."

"So then I kept looking and trying to find you guys."

"Sorry."

"It's not your fault. I was stupid for biking in the rain and I was stupid for faking sick and making you mad at me. I was trying to get to your game to make

46

it up to you. And now you're going to be at school again tomorrow all by yourself, so you're going to get more mad at me. At least this time, I really am sick."

"I do forgive you. I'm still kind of mad, but I get where you're coming from. You were trying to be a good friend. You didn't get sick on purpose."

"Gracias, amiga."

"Samm. You're still here?" Alex's mother came in with a thermometer and a cup of medicine. "You should probably get home. Alejandro needs his rest and you don't need to catch this nasty bug. Missing two days of school." Alex's mother shook her head and clucked her tongue in a display of her disappointment.

"I'll try to get better fast, Samm." Alex said feebly. "I kinda owe you now."

"And you better bet I will collect." Samm said with a grin. She turned to leave. "Bye, Mrs. Cervantes. Thanks for letting me come over."

"Of course, Samantha. You do so much good for Alejandro."

Samm and Alex winced at the use of their full names. Samm recovered before Alex did.

"*Adios, amigo*. Feel better."

"*Adios, amiga*." Alex lifted a hand to her, then closed his eyes while his mother worried over him.

The Vacant Lot

Samm made it through Monday and Tuesday without Alex, but she was happy when he joined her on Wednesday morning and on Friday she made him promise to get up early to go exploring with her on Saturday.

Despite his sickbed promises, he was not a happy ray of sunshine when she roused him bright and early Saturday morning and waited impatiently while he had his breakfast. In fact, he was a grumbling mess of unkempt hair and eyes crusted with sleep. Samm threatened to dump a bucket of water on his head to improve his mood, his appearance, or both. Mrs. Cervantes offered to help.

The night before, Samm had dreamt about taking Alex to the Future-shroom. In the dream, he explained some silly misunderstanding, though Alex could not remember what it was, and everything was back to normal. That was all she wanted – for everything to return to normal. So she begged Alex to hurry.

"C'mon Alex! Let's go!"

"Samm, I could make you a plate, too."

"No, thank you, Mrs. Cervantes. I ate before I came."

"So where are you headed so early this morning?"

"I want to show him where we went on our field trip."

"Is it open on Saturdays? Maybe one Saturday we could all go."

Samm frowned. "Actually, I'm not sure it will be open. Their Facebook page isn't current. I was talking to a classmate that said they were sometimes open on Saturdays, and I told Alex he owed me."

Alex's mother smiled. "Well, I'd rather have him biking to a museum with you in the sunshine than playing video games inside all day. If I took him to a museum, he might sulk the whole time. Unless you'd rather go shopping with me, Alex? I'm heading to the mall after I wash up the breakfast dishes. You could use some new pants."

"Samm needs me. I better go with her." Alex said a little too quickly.

Samm let out the breath she didn't realize she'd been holding, and forced a giggle. "Oh, Alex, if you must go get new pants, I suppose I could go by myself."

When Mrs. Cervantes laughed, too, Samm relaxed and her laugh came naturally. They both knew how Alex felt about going to the mall to shop for clothes.

"There is no love for Alex this morning." Alex pouted.

"Oh, *muchacho*. You know we tease you out of love." Mrs. Cervantes leaned over to kiss her son's head.

"Yuck. I know. I know." Alex tried to dodge, but Samm wasn't sure he was trying very hard. Everyone was grinning. Samm was happy to be treated as one of the family.

She was happier still when Alex finally finished his breakfast, finally finished his chores, and they finally got on the road to A Muse Meant.

"Are you going to tell me what that was all about?" Alex asked as they mounted their bikes.

"What do you mean?" Samm asked. Meanwhile, she was trying to see her destination in her mind. *Left? Or right?* But she couldn't think of directions and evade Alex's questions. She started toward school. Hopefully, the familiar landmark would help her find her way.

"I mean – you lied to my mother." Alex pedaled hard to catch up to Samm, since he had no idea where she might really be going. "Are we just going to school?"

"School first. I didn't lie." Samm spoke as though she were out of breath.

"What 'classmate' told you the field trip place was open today?" Alex put a sneering emphasis on the word.

Samm felt her ears turn red. "Just a classmate. I can't remember who exactly."

"Liar."

Samm started to protest, but she knew she was caught. She just kept pedaling.

They stopped in front of the bike rack at school. Samm tried to look both ways and remember the bus trip in her mind. It hadn't been that far, but it had been a while ago. And she stunk at directions.

Alex looked at her and wiped sweat off his brow with an arm. "So where are we going?"

"I told you."

"No, where are we *really* going?"

"We're going to that field trip place – at the old school. I think it's this way." Samm turned her bike to the right.

"The old school that was on High Street?"

"Yeah."

"That was torn down?"

"It wasn't torn down when we went there."

"I passed it on the way to the soccer fields. It's just an empty lot."

"Well, that can't be it. It was at least three stories."

"Yeah, the old building was. But now it's an empty lot. Some of the guys play hackey sack over there."

"Are you sure?"

"Pretty sure."

"Then where did I go for the field trip?"

"I don't know, Samm. I wasn't there, remember?"

Could it have been another school? A different place?

"Take me to the old lot anyway. Maybe they tore down one building, but our field trip was in another building close by and I'll recognize it."

"Fine by me." Alex shrugged amicably. He might rather be playing video games, but he'd rather be riding his bike with Samm than home doing chores or out shopping with his mother. He pushed down on his upper bike pedal, and they took off.

Not long later, Alex skidded to a stop in front of an abandoned lot. Clumps of scrawny grass broke through the concrete. Samm could see broken brown glass of old beer bottles in several areas where someone might have set them up for target practice. She knew that some poor kids played baseball or soccer in places like this, and was grateful that her community built the ball fields she ran and played her heart out on. Aside from that, though, the lot just made her feel sad – like something precious had been lost.

In a voice that was very small and childish, however, she asked, "why are we stopped?"

"We're here." Alex said. "This is the lot where the high school used to be."

She knew Alex had a very good sense of direction. If this is where he thought the old high school had been, then this was where the old high school had been.

"Could I have been wrong? Could the trip have been somewhere else? We went by bus – maybe it was further away than I thought?"

No building in view looked like the one in her mind, and nothing resembled anything more than familiar neighborhood surroundings. Samm must have ridden past these buildings hundreds of times as a bus and car passenger. But during the field trip, she'd been staring so hard at the doors of A Muse Meant that she hadn't given any thought to her surroundings. It was a problem. Her ability to focus closely on the problem in front of her often meant not seeing what was going on around her.

"They could have had a portable building." Alex reasoned. "They have all those hurricane trailers. They could even make a box of them and throw a roof over so you thought you were in hallways and a bigger space."

Samm tried to think. Reflexively, she wiped her hand on her pants. No, she reasoned. She had been in a three story building. But where was it?

"Let's bike around the block or something." She suggested. "Maybe they changed the location at the last minute, or had something open up. I will know it if I see it, and you really ought to at least see it."

"You're the boss." Alex said.

Samm grinned and took off. She knew she could find it. Alex would understand very soon.

***

"It's not here." Alex said, wiping the sweat from his brow. "We've been circling for hours. But this lot is just a lot. It's not a museum. Sorry, Samm."

"It's gotta be here!" Samm exclaimed. She was hot and miserable. It was getting late and it was hard to talk and pedal at the same time. "It's just gotta be. How do you just lose a three story museum?"

Alex was frustrated, "I've never seen it, Samm – remember? And I don't know what the big deal is anyway. You've never cared about museums before. I saw the Facebook page. It was lame. So what is there? What is the big deal? Somebody added confetti to the baking soda volcano, maybe? Or what?"

"Nothing like that. This museum is just different. I promise. I can't explain it. Just wait 'til you see it!"

"It's getting late, Samm. Our parents are going to worry."

"Not if we find a phone and we call them."

"So where are you going to find a phone in the middle of nowhere? Huh?"

"There!" Samm pointed. Sure enough, there was a pay phone they had not noticed before, in the corner of the abandoned lot they had been circling.

"OK. So you found a pay phone. How're you going to PAY for it?" Alex asked. But inwardly, he was surprised to see the phone at all.

Most adults and teenagers had cell phones, so pay phones were disappearing from public spaces. He and Samm had tried repeatedly to talk their parents into letting them have their own phones. Samm's parents said no because they were worried about the added expense. His said no because they didn't think he was old enough or responsible enough. It just occurred to him that if he asked, his mother would probably buy Samm one just to help keep tabs on him. On second thought, he didn't want to think about how true that might be.

He stepped off his bike and walked it over to where Samm had dropped hers.

Samm had abandoned her bike and was already halfway to the old box. "We're in luck. Two quarters in the coin slot."

"A call costs thirty-five cents now. We only have enough for one call."

"So we call my mom and ask her to call your mom. Problem solved."

Alex couldn't argue. Samm called her parents.

The conversation was very short, but then it didn't need to be long. Alex marveled at the way Samm had her folks wrapped around her little finger. It wasn't as though his were strict, but he had to work just a little bit harder to get his way than she did – except for the computer stuff.

"Thanks, Mommy! Love ya – bye!" She hung up the phone. "We're all set. We've got forty-five more minutes and then we have to be home."

"Well, we don't have any places left to explore. Let's head on back."

"We could just hang out a while." Samm said.

"We could, you know, talk or something."

"Talk?"

"You know, talk. People open and close their mouths and express ideas and opinions about stuff."

58

"Uh – I like milk – cows are great?"

"Ha Ha. Very funny. No, like, just," Samm wasn't sure what she wanted him to say. The Future-shroom was supposed to help her with this conversation, though she didn't want that to happen, either. "Just like, — uhm — You aren't planning to move anytime soon, are you?"

"Well, Dad's job moves him around a lot."

"Yeah, I know."

"And we haven't moved since we got here because he's traveled and Mom and I have stayed behind."

"Yeah?"

"But no, I'm not moving that I know of right now."

"You're not?"

"And Mom kinda sucks at keeping things from me, so I don't think we need to worry about that."

"Good."

"So that's what you wanted to talk about? Did you think I was moving or something?"

"I just wanted to see if you were, is all."

Alex pretended to study his watch.

"What are you looking at?"

"Two minutes and thirty-two seconds."

"Two minutes and thirty-two seconds?"

"Two minutes and thirty-two seconds. Of our forty-five minutes. For you to learn that I'm not planning to move."

"Oh."

"You know, if you want to ask me something, you can just ask me something. You don't have to make up a fake place or act like a lame place is cool or anything."

"Well, yeah, of course." Samm replied with more confidence than she felt. Then she realized what he was implying. "But I swear. I'm not making anything up. There's a real place, and I really want you to see it. I could try to explain, but…"

"But what?"

"No, I couldn't. The words wouldn't come out right. I've tried."

"Ok, then. We can check the address – I probably still have my permission slip wadded up in the bottom of my backpack since I didn't need to turn it in. Until then, back to my house?"

"Sure."

60

They rode back to the neighborhood in silence. Samm's mind continued to race. Why couldn't she talk to her best friend about what she had heard?

At his garage, he parted with his typical, "See you tomorrow?"

"I'll be here."

Returning a Goon

The next week passed much like the previous. However, something was different. Samm couldn't quite put her finger on what it was, but she felt it had something to do with A Muse Meant. She couldn't wait until the weekend, when they could go searching for the museum again. She was more anxious about finding A Muse Meant than she was about the championship game. She found herself wondering if she should skip the game, but dismissed that thought from her mind. Her team needed her. The museum and all its wonders would just have to wait.

She'd tried to ask her classmates. She didn't go on the field trip by herself, after all, but the others just remembered going to a portable building where they climbed a dumb rock wall, watched drama geeks try (and fail) to do science experiments like they were magic tricks, and they ended the day with a planetarium movie on VHS. It almost made sense, but Samm hadn't sat through a movie. She had been in a three story building and fallen off the ladder. She knew she had been frightened by a roller coaster of boa constrictors. She knew there had been a strange man and his stranger Goons. She tried to ask her teacher, but he was distracted and never answered her directly. Over time, she became less and less sure of herself.

Alex still met her in the library after school, but he showed up later and later each day. Did he still want to go home with her?

Samm finally made up her mind to go out into the hallway and wait for Alex there. She was so intent on not missing him and everything being normal that he was there a full minute before she even realized he was there.

"Earth to Samm. Come in, Samm."

"Oh, sorry."

"Hey – where were you? You were like ten thousand miles away."

"Just daydreaming. Hey are we going to go?"

"Actually, I was going to ask you earlier. There's these two guys who need a third for three-on-three soccer in gym today. I could use some off-season practice if I'm going to make the playoffs like you did. Do you mind heading home without me?"

"Oh, I didn't. That is, I don't. I don't mind, Alex. No. Go play ball."

Samm thought she sounded so stupid. She hoped Alex didn't notice.

"I mean, I guess if you wanted to stay and watch, but."

"But no. I get it. It'd be awkward to have an audience at your pick-up game. And I'm not exactly the cheerleader type, anyway."

"Samm, you're the best."

"Yeah, no sweat."

Alex turned to join the two taller guys heading toward the gym. "Hey guys, wait up! I'm coming."

"They don't want me hanging around because they think I'm your girlfriend." Samm said quietly. "You'd be so lucky. Or they don't want me to watch because they know I'm better than they are."

Samm shivered. Those thoughts were not like her. What was going on with her lately? She was sure she didn't want Alex to see this side of her. They weren't joined at the hip. They didn't do everything together. She could back to the library and play games on her Facebook page for a while. He couldn't do that. She started to turn around to go back in, and bumped into something.

"Stupid girly. Outta my way."

"Well, excuse me." Samm knew she was acting rudely, but she didn't care. She slung her backpack into the large person invading her personal space. "There's a big hallway here! Use it! Creep!"

Then she smelled him.

He was absolutely fetid. Peanut butter and tuna fish salad with orange juice disgusting.

Disgusting. And familiar. "Hey! I saw you. You were at the field trip."

"Bad girly."

"I'm not sure whether that's an affirmation or just the way you normally greet people, but I'll take it. You're a Goon, aren't you?"

The Goon grunted.

The Goon was foul. Absolutely disgusting. And yet Samm had spent so long thinking she must have imagined her whole experience that she was happy. Happy – to see a Goon.

"I tried to find your home last weekend," she tried telling it.

The Goon backed away from her, leading her away from the library and down the science hallway.

"We tried to find your place. I mean, my friend Alex was with me. We tried. We circled the area around that parking lot for hours."

The Goon grunted again.

"How did you hide it from us? And why?"

Samm reached out a hand to touch the Goon. The Goon flinched and jumped backward.

"No. Girly bad."

"I'm not going to hurt you."

Samm continued reaching. With every inch her hand extended toward the Goon, he seemed that much more out of her reach.

"Bad Girly!" He repeated. Louder this time.

Samm had had about enough of being ignored, left out, or put off.

"I'm not bad!" she shouted at the creature. "You take that back — you mean old Goon!"

A classroom door opened down the hallway, and a teacher stuck her head out. "Samm, is that you? Is everything OK?"

Samm jumped up. "No, I'm fine, Mrs. Peabody. I'm just —" How was she going to explain the Goon?

66

"Were you talking to someone, dear?" Mrs. Peabody took a few steps in the hallway toward Samm. "Is Alex with you? Are the two of you fighting?"

The Goon was making perfectly horrible faces at Mrs. Peabody. Samm couldn't help it. She giggled.

"Did I say something funny, Samm?" Mrs. Peabody came closer. Samm and Alex had both been in her class last semester. "I asked if Alex was fighting with you."

"No. He's playing three on three in the gym."

"Honestly, that boy… So what are you doing here all by yourself? And what is that smell?"

Samm looked at the Goon and back at Mrs. Peabody. "Hmmm. I'm not sure. Maybe an experiment in the lab?"

"Must be." Mrs. Peabody agreed — perhaps too quickly. "Now Samm, you really need to run along. The library, gym, and cafeteria will stay open until five thirty, but we expect the hallways to be clear of students by now. You need to figure out where you're going and get there."

"Yes, ma'am. I'll go to the library." Samm was torn between wanting to stay with the Goon and being glad to have a reason to leave it behind.

But as she walked away from Mrs. Peabody, the Goon followed her. Mrs. Peabody didn't seem to notice.

"All right, Samm. You have a good afternoon." Mrs. Peabody wiggled her nose, as if trying to shake pollen from it.

"Bye, Mrs. Peabody."

Mrs. Peabody's classroom door shut once again.

Samm turned back to the Goon. "Why didn't she see you?"

The Goon said nothing, just grunted again.

"Well, that's articulate."

The Goon growled.

"You don't scare me. You're just a big ugly Goon."

"You bad girly. You go away."

"Take me with you. To the magic house."

"Magic." The Goon turned away.

"Wait!" Samm cried. "Take me with you."

"No! Bad girly!"

68

A MUSE MEANT

Samm had gone to the Goon and put one hand on his arm. She turned the hulking figure around to face her, and put her other hand on his opposite arm.

"Please, take me to A Muse Meant."

And then they were gone.

***

"Well, hello again, Samantha. Thank you for returning my Goon to me. What an unexpected surprise." Samm recognized the voice of Mr. Rios, the strange man who had led her on the museum tour during the field trip.

Samm blinked and let go of the Goon's arms. She was in a school, but this was an older one.

"Where am I?"

"You remember your field trip, young lady." Mr. Rios said. "This part of the building was not part of your tour. Think of it as the administrative offices."

Samantha blinked and saw rows and rows of cubicles and lateral filing cabinets. She blinked again and saw a classroom. She blinked again and saw the classroom again – but this time with a cauldron filled to the top with bubbling green liquid. She closed her eyes tight, opened them again, and focused on the classroom and Mr. Rios.

"There's nothing wrong with your vision, young Samantha." Mr. Rios assured. "Everything you see is true."

"Impossible."

"Not at all. You see," Mr. Rios laughed at his choice of phrase, "you SEE A Muse Meant for what it really is. You make it even better than I could have imagined – especially on a teacher's salary. This building was abandoned for many years before they tore it down. It was the backdrop for many hopes and dreams and destinies."

"It was just a school."

"Not to someone like you, Samantha. Not to someone who works hard, someone who wishes and dares to dream. Not to someone who has potential. For you it is a wonderful place, though perhaps not as wonderful as another place I could show you."

Mr. Rios snapped his fingers and green smoke filled the room. Samantha started to choke and cough.

"Just relax, Samantha. Breathe it in. I'll take you to a wonderful place. I just know you'll love it. Breathe, Samantha. Don't be afraid. Relax."

Mr. Rios' words did not have a calming effect. She squeezed her eyes shut tight, too, not daring to blink and see what was going on around her. She tried to hold her breath instead, and covered her nose and mouth with her shirt and hands, like she was trying to escape a fire.

But there was no clean air to breathe.

"Relax Samantha. What do you want?"

She wanted to breathe. Her lungs were bursting from lack of oxygen. But she didn't know what was in the green vapor. She didn't want to be a Goon, if that was what Mr. Rios was going to do to her. Why hadn't she just gone home? Why was she always having to satisfy her curiosity? Why couldn't she be with Alex?

"Just think of a place where you feel safe and calm. You don't have to stay with me, Samantha. You always have a choice. Go where you feel safe. I will see you again soon, whatever you decide. Be well, Samantha. Be well."

Unable to breathe, Samm lowered herself to the floor. She had to find some clean air. Had she noticed a door when she arrived? Since she did not remember seeing one, she hoped there had been one behind her. Maybe she could find a doorway. Eyes still shut, shirt and hand still over her mouth, though one hand dropped to the floor to aid her balance, Samm tried half-scooting, half-crawling backwards, trying to use her feet to feel around for a door. She wanted air. She had to get air.

Safe Place

"Samantha? What are you doing here?"

It was a woman's voice. Samm recognized it. She opened her eyes. She was back at her school, in the library. Mrs. Darling the librarian was leaning over her.

"Samm, are you all right? Did you fall asleep back here? It's very late. If I hadn't had a meeting, you might have been locked in for the night. Then what would your parents say?"

She hadn't dreamt it, had she? She really had gone with the Goon to the other school and she really had woken up here. She wasn't crazy.

"Can I call my mom? I don't think I feel well."

"Of course, Samm. You don't look like you feel well. You must have fallen asleep. Where's Alex?"

"He was playing in the gym after school."

"Well, that explains it. You came here to wait for him and then fell asleep. Kids have so much going on these days, they just don't get any time to relax and enjoy it."

Mrs. Darling didn't seem to be talking to Samm directly, so Samm didn't respond. She just followed Mrs. Darling to the office to use the phone.

"He's not all bad, you know. You probably would have ended up in a library either way."

Samm looked at Mrs. Darling. Had she said what Samm heard? Or had she just imagined it?

"Oh, Samm. If there's something going on between you and Alex, I hope you'll talk to him about it. I can tell there's some odd stuff going on between the two of you."

Just dreamed it. Imagined it. Whatever. Mrs. Darling did not really know where she'd been.

"He's not a bad guy, Samm. You just need to get to know him."

"I do know Alex."

"He doesn't know you like I do."

"Are we talking about Alex?"

Mrs. Darling just looked back and smiled. "You'll know when you're ready. Growing up is never easy. But it is worth it."

A MUSE MEANT

Samm was more confused than ever, but she sat down at the deck with the phone and started to dial. Then she looked up at the clock. She had a lot of explaining to do.

***

"What were you doing in the library, Samm?" Alex was asking on the phone later that night. "Your mom even called mine over here. They were both really worried."

"Well, you were playing with those other guys. Weren't they worried about you?"

"Uh – I remembered to call first? Like you usually do when plans change or you're going to be late? I went to the office and called before I ran into you."

"I didn't plan to fall asleep in the library. It just happened."

She didn't know what to say to Alex. She tried to convince herself that it WAS just a bad dream. She could ask him about that.

"Hey, Alex?"

"Yeah?"

"Was I already in the library when you told me about playing soccer?"

"No. Well, sort of. Wait. Let me think. Uhm – you were just outside the library when I saw you, but you said you were going to go back in. Probably to play on your Facebook page, but you didn't say that and I didn't ask. I was thinking about the guys. But when I got there, you were staring off into space like you were really thinking about something. Why do you ask?"

"I guess I was feeling worse than I thought. I went to play" Oh crap. She didn't want to rub in that she had intended to get on her Facebook page, since he couldn't. Not to mention that she didn't actually do that – or at least, she didn't remember logging back on. She quickly amended her story to, "Solitaire on the computer, but Mrs. Darling woke me up in the Rs."

"In the Rs?" Alex started to laugh a little.

"Yeah. Books whose authors start with the letter R."

"Like who?"

Like Rios, Samm thought. But she didn't say that. Luckily, she knew her library. "Rowling, Roth, Ryan, Riordan – lots of good fantasy and dystopian writers."

"So, at least you were in good company." Alex laughed.

Samm laughed, too.

"Are you feeling better now?" Alex asked.

"Yeah. I guess I was just more tired than I thought. I really didn't mean to worry everybody." And now there's no way I can tell Alex about A Muse Meant. He'd never believe me. I don't believe me, and I went there. Twice!

"Don't worry about worrying me. Worry about getting enough sleep. Do you want to skip looking for your magic place this Saturday?"

"Not a chance."

"Even though you're playing in the championship game, too?"

"Yup."

"Good. Because I think I have an idea."

"Really? What is it?"

"I'll tell you tomorrow."

"Alex!"

"So maybe you aren't exactly forgiven for worrying me yet. I'll tell you my plan tomorrow, but that's ONLY if I can tell you're had a good night's sleep. So you better get to bed, Samantha." Alex drew out her name and accentuated it like their parents would.

Samm did not appreciate Alex lecturing her like one of her parents, even if she wasn't being honest with any of them.

"Alex, I slept at school. I'm wide awake now. And now I'm curious about your idea. How do you expect me to sleep tonight?"

"Honestly – not my problem." Samm could tell Alex was suppressing laughter.

"You're so mean, Alex."

"Yeah? Well? Bye!"

Alex hung up the phone. Samm sat there for a few long minutes, and then she hung up the phone as well. What was Alex's brilliant idea? And why would he make her wait all night to tell her?

A MUSE MEANT

***

Samm tossed and turned all night. She dreamt of covering her face to avoid the green fumes. In some dreams, she didn't cover her face, and she and the mysterious Mr. Rios traveled the school on a magic carpet. Sometimes she was there with Alex. In her dream, she wanted to show him the Future-shroom, but couldn't get him off the Boa Coaster.

"Do you like roller coasters?" She asked him the next day on their way to school. On top of everything else, her bike tire was flat this morning, and rather than air it up, the pair was just walking to school. Walking made it easier to talk, so Samm didn't mind that.

"Don't know. Never been on one. Sounds cool."

"You don't think it would make you sick?"

"Isn't barfing on a roller coaster supposed to be part of the fun?"

"Only a boy would think that barfing was fun."

"Only a girl wouldn't agree." Alex retorted.

"Fair point. You win."

"That was fast. You never let me win."

"Sure I do."

"OK. Name one time."

"I just said, 'fair point, you win.'"

"OK, name another time."

"Actually, I'd rather find out your absolutely brilliant idea for finding the field trip place."

"Nope. Your eyes are all puffy. You did not get enough sleep last night."

"Alex! That's because you left me hanging! I swear, I will not"

"*Calmate, chica.* You may be thirteen, but you're going to have the blood pressure of an old man if you don't learn to relax."

Relax. That was what Mr. Rios had told her to do. How could Alex know that?

Samm froze in place. A few steps later, Alex noticed.

He turned around. "Hey, why did you stop? Samm?"

He walked back to her. "Samm, is everything OK? Are you sick for real? Do I need to walk you back home? You didn't catch my bug did you? That was ages ago, anyway."

80

Samm looked up at him, and shook her head to clear it. "No. I'm fine. I stopped because I thought I forgot something, but I'm fine."

"You sure?"

"Of course I'm sure," Samm lied.

"So you're good, yes?"

"Yes, I'm fine, Alex. Geez. Can't I stop in the middle of the sidewalk or anything without getting the third degree?"

Alex tilted his head to the side, rather like confused dogs do when their owner says "fetch," but hides the stick behind their back instead of throwing it. "Don't have to bite my head off," he mumbled. Then he got very interested in something on the sidewalk.

"Look." Samm paused. "Sorry. Alex; I'm sorry. I don't know why I yelled like that."

"It's fine," Alex mumbled, still deeply interested in whatever it was on the sidewalk that was easier to look at than she was.

"You sure?"

"Of course." Alex kicked a rock down the sidewalk, then looked up at her and grinned. "After all, now I have a reason not to tell you my plan until after school."

"Alex! You're making me crazy!"

"I know."

"It's not funny!"

"But it sure is fun."

Samm tried to swipe at Alex with her backpack, but he dodged and started running to the school. Hastily, she followed. The run did both of them good. They arrived at school breathless and laughing.

The Dead Man in the Yearbook

After school, Alex was uncharacteristically waiting for Samm at the library doors. Mrs. Darling had sent her to deliver a hold request to a teacher, so she wasn't back before the ending bell as she'd expected.

"How did you get here so fast?" Samm asked.

Alex's face was all feigned innocence. "What are you talking about?"

"I can't remember the last time you beat me here after school."

"Well, maybe your age is making you slow, *abuelita*."

"Oh, that's cold, Alex. 'Little grandmother,' really?"

"Do you want to argue with me about how slow you are or do you want to come inside and hear my wonderful plan?"

Samm frowned. "Both."

"Nuh uh uh." Alex sing-songed, wagging his finger disapprovingly.

"Fine. Plan."

"Then follow me."

Alex pushed the door open and bowed. Samm hurried inside before anyone could see his silly antic. Bowing, really?

"So what's this great plan you have?"

"Shh! Whisper in the library." Alex said with a Cheshire-cat grin.

"What is your great plan?" Samm stage-whispered as loudly as she dared.

But Alex wouldn't say. He just let her to the reference section. From there, he went to the stack of tall blue yearbooks, selected one, and opened it.

"What are you doing?"

Alex didn't answer her. He flipped to the index, searched it, and then started flipping backwards through the pages. He stopped and turned the book towards Samm.

Samm looked down at the yearbook to see a three-story building. The article title was "Students Say Goodbye."

"Is this…?"

Alex nodded. "This is the building the year it changed from being classrooms to being office spaces. See? There's even an address."

"OK."

"And it's right where you took me – the empty parking lot."

"So?"

"So first of all, your sense of direction doesn't completely suck."

"Gee, thanks."

"No, I'm kidding. It means that there's something going on. Which is probably why you won't tell me about the field trip but want me to find the building with you. It's a mystery, right? Where did they move the building? Unless you went into a building on wheels, we shouldn't have seen an empty lot. There shouldn't have been a pay phone. But I can't figure out what you're not telling me."

Samm put her hand on the page like a bookmark, then flipped back to the index. "Rios, Rios, Rios." She looked up.

"Who are you looking for?"

"Mr. Rios. Uh, a teacher. He isn't listed."

Alex found the teacher section and handed the book back to Samm. She looked at every picture. None looked close to the man she had twice encountered.

"Well, you know what they say. If you don't know, ask. So let's go ask a librarian."

***

Alex steered Samm to the librarian's desk. There, Mrs. Darling, the librarian, was having coffee with a heavy-set man in a janitor's uniform. He had a permanent scowl etched into his face.

"What do you kids want?" He growled.

"Peter, this is Samantha – who goes by Samm — and her friend Alex. They're good students."

"Bah. Heard that before." The man said. Samm was instantly reminded of Mr. Rios's Goons. *"They took care of me,"* he'd said. She wondered what he'd meant by that.

"You got a staring problem, girly?"

Was this guy a Goon? Samm wondered. She bit back a sharp reply, and turned her attention to the librarian.

"We want to find out about Mr. Rios," she said. "You know, the director of A Muse Meant."

The librarian frowned. "Well, I don't know any amusement park directors."

"Not amusement," Samantha clarified. "A Muse Meant. Three words. It's a museum and curiosity shop. Or it was supposed to be. We went there for a field trip. I mean, our class did, but Alex was sick and didn't get to go. I wanted him to see —" Samm wasn't sure what she should admit, either to an adult or in front of Alex – "stuff. But the other students say—"

"Moira — you said they wouldn't see anything!"

"They didn't, Peter. Well, most of them didn't."

"What are you talking about?" Samantha asked. Something really funny was going on.

The heavy-set man reached around behind the librarian and grabbed a high school yearbook from the non-circulating shelf. He muttered while flipping through pages, and came to a stop in the faculty section. "You saw this guy, right, girly?"

"She goes by Samm. Please stop calling her 'girly.' It makes you sound like one of them."

"Like one of who?" Alex wanted to know.

Samm wasn't paying attention, because hers was fixed on the portrait Peter had placed in front of her. The man was pointing to a picture of the man she knew as Mr. Rios, but the caption read "in memoriam" and a name she did not recognize.

"In memory?" She looked at the man. "Does that mean he's dead?"

"A few years ago." The heavy-set man appeared angry. "Just after he announced his retirement."

"Peter – they're just children. This happened at the high school. Do you really think —"

"They won't stay children — not for long, Moira. She's already not, and the boy knows it. But what someone should tell them is that *no good comes from meddling*. Or even trying to do the right thing. Helping students. They should know that good people die and bad things happen to good people."

88

A MUSE MEANT

"How did Mr. Rios die, sir?" Alex asked. He noticed the way Samm froze. He wondered what was so special about this place. He had half thought Samm was making it up to get back at him. Especially when everyone else he talked to just said the field trip had been boring. But Samm was not a good liar. She never had been.

Samm's mind was racing for different reasons. Mrs. Darling knew something. This man called her girly like the Goons did.

"There was a student. A senior. Your 'Mr. Rios' was his advisor. He was a smart kid – had a lotta potential. But he cheated, you see – he cheated on his ACT. And he got caught. They had a meeting to discuss what was going to happen. Odin spoke on the kid's behalf, said it was just too much stress and emphasized what a good kid the young man was. But the others wanted – they thought they needed – to make an example out of him. Odin tried to break the news to the kid gently. And the kid seemed to understand. We didn't see him for a few days. Even wondered if he might go home and kill himself – which I wish he had."

"Peter!" The librarian rebuked.

"Sorry, Moira, it's the truth."

"Sir, how do you know what happened?"

"I was working over there. I was a janitor. After Odin died, I transferred over here. Hoped middle school would be safer. Most of you are kids who aren't thinking about college yet. Most of you, anyway." He looked pointedly at Samm.

She gulped. She'd never felt bad about thinking about the future before, but she did now. Life was strange.

"So, I'm guessing he didn't go home and kill himself," Alex said. "What happened instead?"

"Ah – you can guess."

"We'd rather hear it from you, sir." Alex said.

As if on cue, the janitor's walky-talky started to squawk. "Break's over. Catch you kids later." The janitor strode to the door, but turned again just as his hand was on the security bar. "Moira – I mean, Mrs. Darling – don't baby 'em, now. Hear?"

Alex had seen Mrs. Darling's face relax when the walky-talky went off, and tense up again with the janitor's warning. But Peter left without waiting for Mrs. Darling to reply. Alex heard the door bang behind him as he watched the color drain from and return to the librarian's face.

"What the heck is going on, Mrs. D?"

"Oh, dear. It was a long time ago, Alex."

"But your friend said it was just a few years ago."

"Maybe you should ask your parents to tell you about it."

"How would they know what happened? Was it on the news?" Alex asked, but he was distracted. The whole time, Alex noticed that Samm was still just sitting there, staring at the man in the picture. He didn't look all that special. He was an old white guy with a wreath of fluffy hair circling a bald pate. He had a goatee that reminded Alex of Tony Stark's, but on a man that was much older. This man's hair was not gray; every inch of it was white. Alex could picture him at a poetry reading or a jazz club – what had his English teacher called that group? – Bee's nests? Knick Knacks?

"Beatniks!" Alex exclaimed.

Samm broke from her reverie and looked up. "What did you say?"

Poor Mrs. Darling

What had he said? Alex himself had nearly forgotten. "Oh, right! Beatnik! That's what the old guy looks like."

"You know, I do believe you're right, Alex!" Mrs. Darling said, closing the yearbook so fast Alex almost forgot that they had been looking at someone inside. "Oh, and what fascinating people the Beatniks were." She took the yearbook and placed it on a cart behind the check-out desk Alex and Samm had no choice but to follow. Alex was curious why she put the yearbook out of their reach. Samm seemed to have forgotten all about it. "Oh, the Beatniks were a fascinating group. The Hippies were kind of like the Beatniks. Have you studied about them at all? Simply fascinating."

Alex shook his head. What was Mrs. Darling saying? She was talking about some kind of poetry and pulling out some books in the eight hundreds.

Samm seemed to know what she was talking about, interjecting at all the right points just as she always did.

But something wasn't right. They had been talking about someone. Someone that had died. The dead man in the yearbook! And somehow it was important to Samm. That made it important to him. And now they weren't talking about that man. Mrs. Darling was talking too fast — the way mothers did when they intended to distract their kids. And Mrs. Darling didn't tell them how he died – though Alex thought he could guess. He was going to get Samm out of the library and make her tell him everything she had seen on that field trip. He had a feeling Mrs. Darling had said all she was going to, and he didn't look forward to running into Peter the janitor again. He had a yearbook year; he had a face and a name. That was good enough to start.

But Samm was still talking to Mrs. Darling about poetry slams and beatniks.

"Hey, Samm, we need to get home."

"Don't interrupt Mrs. Darling! She's talking about—"

"It doesn't matter, Samm. We need to be getting home."

"Well, Samm, if you need to leave," Mrs. Darling said.

"Yes, we do, Mrs. Darling." Alex said.

"Alex Cervantes, I can't believe you. I told Mrs. Darling I would—"

Alex let the silence hang over them. Mrs. Darling took her stack of books and walked back to the check-out counter. Alex ignored the librarian, keeping his eyes trained on Samm. He knew Samm couldn't remember why she was there. He felt a little strange, and she looked like she felt strange, too. He waited for her to collect her thoughts, but her eyes got a very faraway look in them once the librarian had put rows of bookshelves between them. Finally, he couldn't stand it.

"Shake out of it, Samm! You're acting creepy!" Alex said.

"What?" Samm replied quizzically. "Really, Alex. Just because you don't like poetry as much as I do is no reason for you to be so rude. We didn't have soccer after school today — Coach forgot to reserve the field — so I wanted to catch up with Mrs. Darling. That's not creepy."

"You have an entire class period with Mrs. Darling every day." Alex pointed out, trying to use logic like Samm would. Her eyes still looked glassy, like she was looking at him but seeing something else.

"But classes are coming in to work on reports. She doesn't have time for me during school. And I really did need help on my poetry project."

"Is that why you think you went to the library? Alex was really confused. "To catch up with a teacher? To work on a homework project?"

"Well, yeah. I was looking for the right book for my report."

Alex could not believe his ears. What on earth was going on? "There is no report, Samm! We went in there to find out something about A Muse Meant and your mystery guy."

"Well, yeah, it was fun for me, but amusement? Is that like a vocabulary word or something?"

"Samm, snap out of it! You went to this place. We thought it was supposed to be the lame science center. Other people tell me it was the boring trip I

faked being sick to get out of. But you saw something
else. And you won't – or you can't – tell me, but I
believe you saw something that was the exact
opposite of lame. And you want me to see it for
myself. And that's cool. We spent hours trying to
find it — whatever it was — last weekend. Today,
we find two adults who know something, but they act
all weird about it, and now you're acting like a ditz
queen or something!"

"Ditz queen? Really? You better take that back,
Alex Cervantes!"

Yelling appeared to break whatever trance Samm
had been in. Alex was grateful. But he decided to
press his luck.

"I won't take it back! You're freaking me out,
Samm! Why won't you just tell me what you saw at
that museum? And who is that guy who's got you all
freaked out?" Alex was ready to shake his best friend
if he had to. This was not normal behavior.

"Why are you yelling at me?"

"I don't know!" Alex yelled. He took a deep
breath, and his next words came out at a lower
volume. "I don't know. This whole thing has me

spooked, Samm. You're acting weird. I thought it was just you and some growing up thing. Maybe even you were mad at me. You're not sick, so I don't know if you fell asleep in the library to try to get me in trouble, or what."

"Alex, that's not what hap—"

"And maybe I've been a terrible friend and maybe I did deserve it, and that's what I thought."

"Alex, I'm not mad at you. I'm not trying to punish you. I don't—"

"I know that now. As of about ten minutes ago. Whatever is going on, I think we have to get to the bottom of it. Something happened to you. And now you're keeping secrets from me. That is way not cool."

"You were the one who said the field trip would be lame. You faked being sick and I went all by myself."

"You didn't go by yourself — you went with our whole class."

"But I'm not like you. No one else will talk to me except you and the teachers."

"So are you telling me you made it all up, Samm? That you had a lame terrible time like I predicted, and then tried to make something interesting out of it so I'd be jealous?"

"No! Something happened! I swear!"

"So tell me! What happened?"

Samm pleaded at Alex with her eyes. Tears threatened to roll.

Alex took a deep breath.

"OK. You can't tell me. Maybe I can get that. If the teacher who led the field trip was as mean as that janitor, and if he threatened you, I guess I can really understand. But if you're hurt – if someone hurt you – we can tell somebody."

"No! It's not like that. It's us. You and me."

"I didn't even go, Samm. I wasn't there."

"But you were there. I heard you talking to me."

"I was home in bed, Samm."

"I know. That's why I want to show you."

"Show me what?"

"Something crazy. Something I don't understand."

"So tell me what you know and maybe we can understand it together."

"It's like a dream, Alex, but it was real. I absolutely remember it. I remember the way I felt when I was there. But I can't explain it. Like maybe it's on the tip of my tongue or I dreamed it in another language and I just don't have the words for it. But it's about you. So I can't not tell you. And then nobody else saw anything. So I thought maybe it was just me. And then a Goon showed up at school."

"What? You didn't tell me that! What's a Goon?"

"Like the janitor, but uglier."

"Ugh."

"You have no idea."

"Ok. Well, you're my best friend, and it's important to you, so it's important to me. We'll find it. We'll find this Goon-thing, whatever it is."

"And what happens when we do? That janitor told us that the man I was talking to has been dead for years. I left the library and I forgot about him. I just forgot, Alex. How does that happen?"

"I know, Samm. It's really weird. But we'll find the place. We'll find the place, and you'll get your answers."

"Together."

"Of course, Samm."

"But these things I see – they've only happened when we aren't together. When I think I'm alone."

"We definitely need to talk to Mrs. Darling again – when that creepy janitor isn't around. But you're not alone. We're going to figure this out. OK?"

"OK."

"Let's go home."

The Big Game

Samm's team took the field against the champions from the eastern part of the state. Alex couldn't remember their team name. But Samm had reminded him that they had met earlier in the season and been victorious, so they were pretty confident.

Alex stood beside the coach. Parents lined up on both sides of the field in lawn chairs or standing. There was a set of bleachers on the guest side of the playing field, but they sat empty. For a championship game, Alex thought, there should be more fans.

Maybe the low turnout had to do with how early it was on a Saturday? He kinda wished he drank coffee. He opened his water bottle and took a swig. He had to be careful not to drink too much, because the restroom facilities were not close by. It was a pain.

Alex watched Samm take her place slightly in front of midfield. She enjoyed making plays from this position. She told him it didn't carry the pressure of being a forward -- which was also typically the position of their team captain. Samm's team captain admired her skill, but wasn't making any effort to replace him as Samm's best friend. Alex thought she was probably a little bit threatened by Samm, even though Samm didn't do anything to be threatening. Samm was above all a team player.

The referee got the forwards to meet in the center of the circle and shake hands. Then they stepped back, and he tossed the ball high into the air. Were there any female referees? Alex wondered. He'd certainly never seen any, not in all of Samm's games. But the girls didn't seem to mind. Their coach was a guy, too. And Alex liked this. He wasn't sure if he could hang out on the sidelines with a lady coach. It was hard enough sometimes to be the only boy their age at the games, and hard when Samm's mom thanked him over and over for showing up.

Samm's captain got a toe on the ball first, and she dropped it back to Samm. Samm passed the ball across the field to the other midfielder. The strategy was a good one. Let everyone get a toe on the ball

102

early on, and make the other team chase the ball from player to player. Ideally, they would wear out, and then Samm's team could score easily.

Alex mentally compared this to the hot doggers who had made up his team. He preferred being a defender, but a lot of guys all tried to be forwards and hog the ball. They'd run halfway down the field with the ball and then they'd get tired at the same time two or three players from the other team would have him cornered. And the guys always thought they could outrun the defenders. Samm's team's more social game had a much better idea.

Alex waved when Samm happened to glance in his direction. She nodded to him and grinned. The other team had a hot dogger for a forward, and Samm and her team had noticed. Now they knew who needed the most defending. Of course, it could be a trick play, but Samm's grin told Alex that she remembered this. As they reached the scoring end of the field, Samm slowed and changed direction to the edge of the field. This way, she had better visibility and could see if the ball would be returned to her attacking position by her team's defenders. The forward stopped just outside the center circle, also waiting.

They didn't have to wait long. The defenders came through. The game remained scoreless. Alex knew the ball could volley back and forth for most of the game, if both sides had good defensive players. Some people liked high scoring games, but Alex could appreciate all the near misses and close calls as the players ran up and down the field.

He looked past the game to the table where Samm's mother had laid out awards and participation trophies. Samm and her mother had argued about them in the van. Samm thought that setting them out before the game would give them bad luck. Samm's mother argued that the coach had bought them for getting to the championship game, so they would get them even if they lost this game. Alex thought both were good points, and had been smart enough not to get between them. But now he could hear Samm's mother cheering. She always sat or stood at the end of the field that Samm would be scoring in during the second half of the game. Alex didn't know why she didn't move her chair for each half, since there was enough time and not too many fans to impede movement. He shrugged. Parents were funny.

Mr. Cisneros was seated beside his wife. He looked on at the game intently, but did not cheer or yell like Samm's mother did. Occasionally, he would clap for a good play. Alex didn't feel like he knew Samm's father very well. Most of the time, he was working. And Samm was at his house more often than he was in hers. His own dad was also gone a lot because of work. Alex's dad was an airline pilot. He tried to be home on Sundays, but that didn't always work out.

Wow! The defenders snagged a ball away from the other team and sent it up in a perfect arc to Samm's team captain. The forward deftly took control of the ball from the center circle, then pivoted and led the ball in breakaway fashion toward the goalie's net. Samm ran up to assist. The goalie and sweeper came forward to meet the challenge. Like they had done so many times in practice, the captain positioned her body to make it look like she was going to pass to Samm. The sweeper moved to Samm to intercept. In the moment where they might have collided, the forward actually kicked the ball behind her to the other midfielder she expected to be waiting there. And she was not disappointed. The other midfielder, seeming to come from out of nowhere, took advantage of the goal and the sweeper's focus on Samm and kicked the ball diagonally into a beautiful goal the goalie recognized too late. The trio high fived each other quickly and then returned to their defensive positions.

Play resumed quickly, and the ball traveled between attacks and defence over and over. Just before the halftime break, a lucky kick by the opposing team's forward tied up the game.

Samm ran off the field and grabbed a water bottle from the cooler. Alex handed her a towel.

"Great first half. That breakaway play was amazing."

"Thanks. Yeah. I hope next time I get the assist, and I wish we were ahead, of course, but it IS the championship game. We're pretty evenly matched."

Samm's mother came up then and hugged her daughter. "*Mija*, we are so proud of you! This match is so exciting to watch."

Mr. Cisneros hung back, clearly uncomfortable around all the teen-aged girls.

Samm finished the bottle of water and handed her towel back to Alex. "Thanks."

The coach called them all to a huddle. Alex was only vaguely paying attention. What could the coach say?

But then he saw Samm jump up, leave the huddle, and run across the field. It was the strangest thing. It was like she was shooing a dog off the field, but there was no dog. Or that she was chasing after a slipped hair ribbon -- but Samm didn't wear ribbons in her hair on the day of the championship game. She just wore an elastic around her ponytail.

Samm's teammates yelled at her to come back. The coach had a worried look on his face. Mr. and Mrs. Cisneros looked on with concern.

Finally, Samm came back.

"What the heck was that about" the coach demanded.

"Uh," Alex could tell Samm was stalling for an excuse. "Uh -- a wasp. Yeah. There was a wasp, and it was on me, and"

Worst possible liar ever. Alex thought. But he could help. "Coach, did you not see it?" he piped up. "I was surprised you weren't all screaming when I saw it land on Samm's jersey. She was thinking quick to get it away from all of you."

The players and coach looked at Alex skeptically.

Samm flashed him a grateful look and mouthed "thank you."

Alex didn't dare mouth back while so much attention was on him, but he knew Samm understood he would have said "you owe me" if he could.

The referee blew the whistle and both teams got back on the field. But instead of being confident and excited, Alex thought Samm looked nervous. She kept looking back to the place where she'd run. Alex decided to walk over there and investigate.

"Not so fast, Alex," said the coach without taking his eyes from the field.

"Yeah, Coach?" Alex replied, somewhat sheepishly.

"Do you know what was really going on with Samm? I need her head in the game."

Alex thought through a couple scenarios in his head, but remained silent.

"OK, then. Keep your secret. I hope it doesn't cost us."

"Yes, Coach."

"And son?"

"Yes, Coach?"

"Thanks for being her friend. I know it can't be easy to be the only guy your age here." Coach took his eyes off the field very quickly to meet Alex's. "And we never had this conversation."

Alex grinned and ducked away quickly. He wasn't sure why they weren't supposed to have had that conversation, but honestly he was more interested in seeing what was on the other side of the field. Aware that the coach probably still had an eye on him, he carefully walked around the field. He wanted to run, but he didn't want to attract more attention and he did kind of want to know how Samm was doing in the game. Her team was not passing the ball to her. He frowned. The other team probably wouldn't notice because the ball was going to everybody — everybody except for Samm.

He passed the goalposts and kept going around. He laid eyes on the trophy table Samm's mom had set up. He hadn't noticed if anyone had been around it during halftime. Maybe that was what Samm had seen.

And then he smelled it. Something foul. He smelled a terrible combination of body odor and cow manure. He looked around. Maybe someone had changed a baby diaper over here and dropped it instead of taking it to a trash can? Maybe -- he looked at the field that was next to the soccer field. Maybe someone's cow got out and dropped some patties near the field? But he looked and looked and didn't see anything.

And because he was looking for the source of the smell, he missed Samm being passed the ball and then being immediately fouled. Penalty kicks came at the end of the game though, so Alex decided to head back to the other side with the coach.

He was crossing the goalposts again when the other team's forward came out of nowhere with the ball. The goalie had been watching Alex and not paying attention.

110

"Watch out!" Alex called.

The forward kicked the ball. It flew toward the goal. However, thanks to Alex's warning, the goalie caught it in the air and cherry-bombed it back across the center circle. The game was still tied one to one.

Both sides made many close calls, but the game would come down to Samm's penalty kick.

Both teams took their places outside the penalty area. Only Samm and the goalie for the other team were inside. All eyes were on Samm. If she could make this kick, her team would win the championship.

Alex could not believe what was happening. In his mind's eye, he saw it. Samm would kick the winning goal. She would be declared the championship game MVP. The other girls on the soccer team would pay her more attention than ever before. He wasn't sure how he felt about that.

Samm took her time setting the ball on the line just where she wanted it. Finally, she nodded to the referee, who asked the goalie if she was ready. the goalie nodded.

The goalie clapped her mitted hands together and then spread her limbs wide. Samm stepped back from the ball, clenched her fists at her sides, then ran forward. As her right foot went to make contact with the ball, Alex noticed her chest jerk backward. Her foot slid over the top of the ball. But she still had forward momentum, so although she had planted her left foot for the kick, her right slid over the top of the ball and she crashed down, sitting on the ball like it was the craziest sort of egg. Alex thought it would have been hilarious if it had happened to anyone but Samm. But there was his best friend, trying to pick herself back up to reattempt the kick.

However, the referee blew the whistle and said that unfortunately, Samm violated the one-touch rule of penalty kicking, so she would not get a second attempt.

Alex could tell that Samm's captain and the coach both wanted to protest the decision, but a tied game was better than a loss, and if they got carded for arguing, the referee could decide to award a penalty kick to the other team. So Alex watched his best friend put on her bravest face, stand in line with her teammates to congratulate the other side, accept the award from the table her mother laid out, say

112

goodbye to her teammates, get to the van, and then, finally, burst into tears.

Alex knew he had to do something to help. And he could only think of one thing that would help his friend. They just had to find that museum. They had to find A Muse Meant.

A Most Unusual Diner

After the disappointing tie, Alex tried to cheer Samm up. So they rode home with Samantha's parents, then got on their bikes to head out again. This time, Samm let him lead, and he led them directly to the lot that was empty the previous week. It was not empty now. It was a diner. The diner was an old tin building that looked like it had been there for years, not days. Its windows were dark tinted glass that Samm could not see inside of. It was too big to have been a food truck wheeled in from somewhere else.

"You hungry?" Alex asked.

"We don't have any money." Samm replied.

"Somehow, I don't think that's going to matter." Alex said. "C'mon. I trust you. Trust me."

Samm took Alex's outstretched hand, and, blushing furiously, allowed him to lead her inside. She had always wanted to go to a diner. She saw a lot of them on TV, but her mother nearly always made meals at home.

The diner looked bigger from the inside. A burly waiter in white clothing led them to a back table without a word.

The two-way mirror allowed them a view of old cars and pick-up trucks outside, like you might expect to see at a vintage drive movie. Samm did not remember seeing the vehicles when they arrived on their bikes. She wondered if the building just had her turned around. Maybe she was looking at the side of the building, instead of the front. Samm wasn't sure. She squeezed Alex's hand.

The diner seemed full of people, but she couldn't concentrate on a single face. They were seated at a booth next to silver swinging doors that presumably led to the kitchen. Samm could hear noises in there, but they were rather fuzzy, like something she might experience in a dream.

At the front counter alongside them was a soda machine, and they could see the man who had waited on them add old fashioned ice cream to two glasses, dispense soda into both, add straws and umbrellas and return to them.

"We didn't order." Samm said.

"Relax. Maybe that's all they offer."

"Then why is there a kitchen?"

"Is it a kitchen?"

"Why wouldn't it be?"

"Do you want to check it out?"

Samm tried to see art on the walls, to get an impression of the theme of this diner, but she couldn't. The images were fuzzy, and again Samm had the impression that she was dreaming rather than truly having this experience. If this was a dream, she wanted to enjoy it.

"Maybe after we have our ice cream sodas."

The treats looked really good. When the waiter put them down on the table, both Alex and Samm took eager sips through their straws.

"Mmmmm. That's the ticket." Alex said.

Samm blinked, and then looked at Alex again across the table. Alex was still Alex, but he was different, too – older.

"Do you remember the first time we came here, Samm?" Older Alex said. "We were just kids."

Samm turned her spoon around to see if she could see her reflection in it. But the distortion was too great to tell.

She asked him, "Alex, how long ago was that – when we were kids?"

"Oh, four or five years, I guess."

"Right."

"Samm, are you feeling OK?"

Samm looked around the room. Instead of happy couples, the diner was mostly vacant. The few people at tables were Goons.

"I think I'm going to be sick."

Samm rushed to get outside. Ice cream and soda clung to her throat, threatening to choke her. Had it been poisoned? She'd read stories about fairies who'd tricked mortals into consuming their food and staying with them forever. But Goons weren't fairies and she certainly didn't want to stay with them.

Older Alex held her hair back while she upchucked into some bushes. It was nice, but extremely weird.

"I've got a water bottle in my truck." He said. "Let me get it for you."

117

Truck? Alex didn't even have his learner's permit. Neither did she. Where were their bikes? But she watched Alex head confidently to an old rust-red pick-up, open the door, and emerge with his water bottle.

"The bottle's old, well, you know that. But it's clean. It's just water. You can rinse your mouth out."

Samm accepted it. "Thanks."

"I guess you'll want me to take you home, since you're not feeling well. We'll see the movie another time."

"Yeah, that would probably be for the best."

Samm walked over to the passenger side of the truck. Alex opened the door for her. She caught herself in the rearview mirror. "That's what I look like?" She said.

Older Alex misunderstood. "You don't look so bad. Maybe you're a little green right now, but I know it will pass. You're still my girl, right?"

Samm was saved the embarrassment of a reply by a Goon with a squee-gee.

"Hey, stop, what are you doing!"

"Window wash. You pay five dollars. I wash."
said the Goon.

"I didn't ask you to wash my window!" Alex
cried, "You need to go away!"

Older Alex fumbled to put his key in the
ignition.

"Window wash. Five dollars." The Goon
repeated.

Older Alex turned on his windshield wipers and
sprayer, which hit the Goon's face and made a loud
hissing sound. The Goon yelled and jumped back.
Other Goons turned toward the sound and Older
Alex's truck. They slowly moved their hulking
bodies towards the vehicle. Just when Samm thought
things couldn't get any worse, she saw a green
reptilian thing coming around from the side of the
building. Was this what Goons became?

"What is going on?" Older Alex beat his hands
on the steering wheel. With the key in the ignition, he
could operate the sprayer and the wiper blades, but he
could not make the engine turn over. "Samm, I don't
understand what's happening."

"You're too young to drive, Alex! We rode our
bikes here!" Samm yelled, petrified that their

armored truck was going to give way and they were going to be sitting ducks on bicycles when the dream faded.

Instead, her shout had a calming effect on her friend, and he let go of the steering wheel and the key. The truck disappeared, but a silvery rainbow haze enveloped the pair and put them back on their respective bikes.

Samm blinked again, and when she opened her eyes, she and Alex were staring at the pay phone in front of an empty lot. The receiver was off the hook. The Goons and the reptile thing were nowhere to be seen.

"Are you OK?" Alex asked.

Samm nodded, not trusting herself to speak.

"I'm going to go hang up the phone. Though I'm pretty sure you used it last."

Alex stepped off his bike, walked the few steps to the pay phone, returned the receiver to the cradle, and walked back to Samm.

"You're shaking." He said.

"Did you see that – before?" Samm asked.

"The diner, the milkshakes, the big ugly guys, and me driving a truck? Yeah. Pretty weird, huh?"

"Pretty weird."

"Samm?"

Samm lifted her eyes to meet his.

"Are you doing all this?"

She was more surprised to hear "I don't know, maybe," escape her lips.

"Well, one thing's obvious."

"What's that?"

"I'm pretty sure we found your A Muse Meant."

PDA in the Library

It was hard leaving the empty lot, but after hours of sitting there, willing it to return to the diner or become the school, the sun began its lazy descent to the western side of the sky, and Alex told Samm it was time for them to go.

"You're tired. We'll come back next week. It won't be an empty lot then. You'll have had a chance to clear your mind. I believe in you."

Samm smiled at Alex, but she knew simple fatigue wasn't her problem. She wasn't sure what she wanted. That WAS a problem. A big problem.

She wanted to see the old school. She didn't want to show Alex the Future-shroom – not anymore. She wanted to return to the diner and have a milkshake that didn't make her sick. She wanted to be able to use the payphone to call someone who would understand. She wanted someone she could pour her heart out to, someone who would hear and not judge, someone who would keep her secrets safe. She remembered when that someone was her parents. Or Alex. A month ago may as well have been a lifetime ago. And now Alex was pushing her to take the lead. Why? She didn't want that. Together. That's how they'd always done things. Part of her wished she'd never gone on that field trip. Wished she had rushed over and caught Alex's cold so they both would have stayed home.

But he hadn't really been sick – she reminded herself again. He had left her alone. Got sick trying to make it up to her – which had made her more alone. Was off with his friends when the Goon found her outside the library. She'd gone with the Goon because Alex had left her alone. She didn't want to be alone. But she didn't want Alex to be a boyfriend or anything like that. What did she want?

Though Mama said wishes weighed nothing, the weight of Samm's conflicted wishes felt heavy on her shoulders. Her hands gripped and un-gripped the handlebars of her bike.

"So, are you going to tell me what happened to you during that final kick?" Alex asked gently.

The soccer game seemed like ages ago. Samm forced herself to think clearly and remember. "What did you see?"

Alex thought back, too. "You were going to make the kick, but then you got shoved backwards. Except I couldn't see what shoved you."

"But you saw something. You don't think I just imagined it, right?"

"Your top half moved backwards before you fell. I saw that."

"Do you remember the things trying to wash the windshield?"

"Yeah."

"They're called Goons. And one of them pushed me."

"Why would he do that?"

"He was going to mess up Mama's table. The wasp thing I said? I was trying to scare him off. But I didn't want Coach to think I was crazy."

"But that was on the opposite side of the field."

"Yeah. I thought it disappeared when I scared it, but I could still smell it. Then it reappeared at the end of the game. I'm not sure why."

Alex thought. "Wait a minute – you could smell it? Was that the awful diaper smell?"

"Oh, I think it's worse than that. We were lucky to be in the truck at the diner."

"Yeah – but no – I wanted to tell you. I smelled it, too. I walked over to where you had been. I thought maybe you dropped a lucky rabbit's foot or something and just realized it."

"Since when have I carried around some kind of good luck charm?"

"Besides me?"

Samm laughed. "Yeah. Besides you."

"I don't know. Maybe you always have and I didn't know."

"Nope. I probably could have used some extra luck though."

"You got some luck. Rotten luck."

Samm wrinkled her nose. "Rotten. Yeah. Thanks for reminding me."

***

The next week at school dragged on. Samm didn't remember most of it. Soccer was over, which was just as well, since the team was pointedly trying to act like she didn't exist. She wrote papers, solved equations, raised her hand and gave answers – all by route. During her appointed library time, she didn't ask to go near the computers. She just sat in the R section and contemplated her choices. What would show up the next time they went to the abandoned lot? What the heck was that reptile doing? Had Alex seen it? She couldn't bear to ask him.

A different English class filed in to the library Friday afternoon. Samm sighed. She had hoped she could be alone with the books. Samm heard Mrs. Darling say, "Remember, you might have to enter several keywords to get to the best information about your topic. Even if you're doing a report on John Paul Jones, there are a lot of people with that name. You need to know something about the John Paul Jones you want to research so you don't end up with a report about a man who's lived six different lives."

Samm laughed at the joke no one else seemed to get, but then she started thinking.

Six. That was how many arms and legs the reptile Samm had seen had. Man. It stood like a man.

126

A MUSE MEANT

Hard to tell at first when its four hands were on the corner wall of the building. A lizard could have climbed straight up the wall, but only a bearded dragon could walk on hind legs like that. So what was it?

"Do you think this green eyeshadow brings out my eyes?"

Samm guessed the seventh grade girl was trying to copy some movie starlet. Samm just thought she sounded silly. And the older girl's lanky boyfriend certainly didn't seem to mind it.

"Looks awesome. Give me the green light, and here I come."

If the young man understood that green meant go, then why was her lipstick red? Samm covered her mouth with her hand before she got caught giggling out loud.

"Shh! She'll notice that we're not with the class."

"That's what makes this fun – when you can get caught!"

Ugh. Only one aisle of shelves in front of her, and they were kissing. Ew. Gross.

She turned to the side so she didn't have to see them. But she was sitting too close to the shelf and knocked over a book with her elbow.

It wasn't very loud, but it was loud enough to break up the kissing couple.

The puppy lovers spied her through spaces in the shelves. "Ew! Little sixth grade freak! You were watching us! You perve!"

"No, I wasn't." Samm stammered. She didn't know why she was feeling nervous. They were the ones that came into her space. But she had been watching them. She was repulsed that a small part of her wanted to BE them.

This was her safe spot, but it wasn't safe anymore. Samm grabbed her backpack and fled – out of the bookshelves, out the doors of the library, out of the hallway, until she was outside the awning in the grass. Here, she sank down, caring but not caring who saw her there. The buses were lined up to take students home after school. She had maybe twenty minutes until this place would be crawling with students.

A MUSE MEANT

Why did they have to use her stacks for their romance? What were boys and girls doing pairing off like that, anyway?

She rubbed her arms. Darn – she'd forgotten her jacket on the back of a computer desk chair.

Samm's thoughts continued to circle the drain between anger at the couple, anger at herself, and self-pity.

When the dismissal bell rang, Samm moved to a secluded corner of the building and hid behind an air-conditioning unit. She watched carefree students laugh and kid with each other as they boarded the buses for the weekend.

"Long week?" Alex didn't seem surprised to have found her.

"I would have come back to the library eventually… Maybe."

"Hey, I don't blame you. Mrs. D. took care of Amy and Max. It wasn't right for them to be hiding out and sucking face."

"Ugh; don't remind me."

"Sorry. Is it better if I say PDA?"

"No."

"Semi-private displays of affection?"

"Not better." Samm blushed, though, and grinned.

Alex smiled back. "Anyway, the face suckers should be embarrassed – not you."

"I wasn't watching them."

"I know. But if you were, what would it matter?"

"Huh?" Samm was confused. Did Alex – was Alex interested in people their age kissing?

"It's like watching a car wreck, or a volcano, isn't it?" Alex explained. "I mean last year, I was playing tag with Max at recess. Now he's sucking face with this seventh grader, and holding her hand all the time. She's got all this make-up on and she thinks she looks like a hot teenager -- but I think she looks like a clown. What do you girls like about that stuff?"

"I don't know, Alex." Samm said, perhaps a little testily. She did not like being thrown in with all the girls. "I don't like that stuff."

"Oh yeah. Right."

"Max is our age. Why was he in the library with the seventh grade class?"

"Probably found out she was going to be there and asked coach for a study pass. Or he just skipped. Coach doesn't seem to care about players missing practice unless they're prepping for JV."

"Oh." Despite the fact that Samm had fled the library and so technically skipped class, too, she couldn't see someone skipping on purpose. She supposed that was another way Max meant "getting caught."

Alex cleared his throat. "So listen – do you want to go back to the library?"

Samm didn't answer right away.

"Or do you just want to go home?"

Samm raised an eyebrow at Alex, and waited. Honestly, she didn't want to think. She wanted someone else to decide.

But Alex just met her gaze and didn't say anything.

Finally, Samm said, "School's out already."

"Do you have your stuff?"

"I have my backpack, but I left my coat on a chair by the computers." She knew she didn't have to say "in the library." They both knew where she left her coat.

"Do you want me to get it for you?"

"Yes, please. I'm not ready to face Mrs. Darling yet. I shouldn't have done nothing. I should have reported them right away."

"You'll see her sooner or later. And you don't have anything to be embarrassed about. I bet Mrs. D. won't even remember it Monday. You weren't the one engaged in PDA."

"Can you not say PDA?"

"But it's so cute when your face gets all pink."

Samm shuddered, and not just from the cold.

Alex laughed and headed back into school. Samm waited a minute, then decided she was cold and ran after Alex anyway. The library was empty with the lights off when they got there, so Samm picked up her coat and they left.

"Are we going exploring this weekend?" Alex asked.

"I plan to."

"Good. I'm kinda craving another milkshake."

They walked home in companionable silence.

Reverse Psychology

Alex's mother was shaking out rugs on the front porch when Samm arrived Saturday morning.

"Another big adventure planned?"

"No. Just another day."

"Hmmm." Mrs. Cervantes was thoughtful. "I hope it warms up for you."

"It's not so bad once we've been biking a while. A little wind is good."

"I guess. I would be perfectly happy with year-round summer though. Like home."

"Where was home for you?"

"Don't you know, Samm?" Alex's mother set the rug on the railing and moved to sit by the porch. She beckoned Samm to join her.

"I forgot." Samm confessed, dismounting from her bike and taking a seat on the wooden porch next to her best friend's mother.

"Oh, it's OK. I'm from Puerto Rico."

"So, uh, did you have to get papers to move here?" It was taboo to ask someone where they were in the citizenship process if they didn't volunteer such information – even your parents. Still, a lot of kids in the Facebook groups talked about their fears and uncertainties. Maybe the Future-shroom was telling her that Alex was being deported.

"No, honey, we don't need papers. Puerto Rico is a US Commonwealth. Puerto Ricans have the same status as US citizens, except they don't vote for President unless they move to a US state."

"Oh. That's cool." So that wasn't it. Samm was relieved, but the question remained – why was Alex telling her he was going away?

"Is everything OK with your family, Samantha?"

Samm knew Mrs. Cervantes was asking about papers because she had asked first. "Oh, yes, I think. I mean, as far as I know." Samm honestly didn't know where her family was in the process.

"You two are putting in a lot of miles on your bikes these Saturdays. Meeting friends?"

"No. Just exploring."

"Well, I love that time Alex spends with you is time he isn't spending playing video games. And I was young. Once. A very, very long time ago. We used to go 'exploring,' too. Before I got old." Alex's mother smiled.

"Mrs. Cervantes, you're not old!"

"Ah, you're a sweet girl. But I'm more than a decade older than I was when Alex was a baby, no? We grow up. We get old. We even get wrinkly. It just means we live."

Samm started to protest, but Alex's mother stopped her.

"It's OK, Samm. I wasn't fishing for compliments. And I know you won't let Alex do anything dumb. I'm really glad you two are still such good friends, you know? I know this can be a hard age for you young people."

Samm didn't know whether Alex's mother was talking in generalities or if she knew something more. Had Alex been talking to his mom about them?

"I trust you to take him 'exploring' and to have grand adventures. Keep as much magic in your lives while you can, for as long as you can, *mija*. If you tell me you're being safe, then I believe it." They could both here Alex coming to the door. Samm's mother was clearly wrapping up the talk she wanted to give. "My *muchacho* would tell me the sky was green if he thought I'd believe it. So of course, I can't trust him."

"Mom!"

Alex and his mother bantered back and forth a little while Samm reflected on what she had just been told. She liked that Alex's mother trusted her, just like Mrs. Darling and her teachers did. She liked that her parents trusted her, too. Was she doing something wrong not telling any of them all she knew about A Muse Meant? Moreover, what did she really know about the lot that held a museum, then was empty, and now was a diner?

"You ready to go Samm?"

Hearing her name brought Samm back to the conversation. "Yeah, yeah, let's go."

"Bye, Mrs. Cervantes!"

"Have fun, both of you. Samm, please take good care of my son."

"Yes, ma'am."

They pedaled a few blocks in silence before Alex broke it.

"So, what was that all about?"

"Hmmm?"

"You and my mother, all buddy-buddy?"

"So? I like your mother."

"She kept saying for you to take care of me. Did you tell her where we were going?"

"No. And she didn't ask. Which was kind of weird, to be honest."

"Yeah. My mom's usually pretty nosy."

"She kept wanting to make sure I knew she trusted me. Have you said something to her?"

"What would I say? She'd think I was making it up. An ice cream shop diner at the site of the old school building? Spending our weekends looking for a building that we know was torn down but you have been in even though you won't tell me about it?"

Samm heard the question he didn't ask, but had one of her own. "I got sick, so I never asked you – what do you remember about the diner?"

"I remember the truck, Samm. I remember you looking at me different. But then you were puking and I thought maybe that was why. Did you get sick during the field trip, too?" Alex put the brake on and stopped short.

137

Samm braked more slowly, turned around, and pedaled back to Alex. "What?"

"Oh, man! Is mom doing that thing when parents say one thing but mean the opposite thing?"

"Are you saying your mom doesn't trust me?"

"Of course not. Mom loves you. Sometimes I think she loves you more than me."

"So what are you saying?"

"Help me with that word – what is it when a parent says something like 'you don't have to eat your dinner – you can go straight to bed' or 'sure you can wear shorts when it's snowing, doesn't everybody?'"

"Reverse psychology?"

"Yeah! That's it! Now where was I going with that?"

"I have no idea. Your mom."

"Yes. Right. Mom was talking to you about how she trusts you to take care of me and how I'm so reckless and everything."

"Yeah?"

138

"What if that was – uh – reverse psychology- to get me to be less reckless and to help take care of you?"

"So why wouldn't your mom just tell you that?"

"Because I'd tell her you're a big girl who takes care of herself."

"Awww, that's sweet. I think."

"Yeah, sometimes I can bring it." Alex puffed out his chest and held his shoulders back. But then his bike shifted underneath him and he had to scramble to set it straight before it knocked him down.

"Talented, too." Samm said, trying to keep a straight face.

"Ah, go away with you," Alex said with a fake scowl.

Samm grinned. "So we're really going back to the diner? Do you think it will still be there?"

"Honestly, I have no idea what to expect." Alex grinned. "And I don't mind so much."

"Me, either." Samm agreed. "I mean, part of me is really freaked out, but I feel better since we found the diner. It's like a big puzzle. Every time we go to that lot we find one more piece. Every Saturday, we move one step closer to A Muse Meant. Maybe today, we'll even find the school."

"I guess we'll know in a minute. You ready?"

"I think so. Yeah, let's do this."

"All right!"

They set off again, not stopping until they reached the familiar lot. But it wasn't empty. The diner was gone. The school, all three stories of it, loomed above them. Alex and Samm turned to one another and grinned.

"Do you see what I see?" Samm asked.

"If you see a three story building, I do."

"I see a three story building."

"There's only one thing missing."

"What's that, Alex?"

"You know those old timey signs like they have for the circus?"

"Yeah."

"I kind of thought this place would have one."

Samm looked at the second story, trying to picture it. "How would they hang it?"

Alex studied the building. "Well, it'd be hard to mount brackets to the brick unless you hired

140

someone, and I don't see your teacher-guy doing that. But maybe he got brackets that he could hang on the third story window, and he could have carried his sign up to the third floor, where he had a guide rope that he used as a pulley, and put the sign on it. Then he'd pull on the pulley to move the sign into position, and there'd be a cord so he could plug the sign in. Woah."

As Alex worked out the logistics, Samm pictured the actions in her mind. When she could see it, Alex could, too.

"Are you doing that, Alex?"

"Uh – I think you are."

They watched as the sign blinked and then flashed on.

"We saw the sign get installed, but I didn't see your mystery man."

"Mr. Rios."

"Yeah, mysterious."

"No. The guy called himself 'Mr. Rios.'"

"Oh." Alex looked at Samm as it dawned on him. "That's why you were hanging out in the Rs."

Samm looked sheepishly back. "Uh huh. Well, I woke up there. It was a mistake."

141

"Because you always hang out at the tables or computers."

"Exactly."

"So where'd you go?"

"When I came here?"

"Yeah."

"There was this white room. And in the front there was a science table – you know the kind in the movies with the sink and the knobs? And it had test tubes on it that looked like some kind of pan flute but glass tubes instead of wood? But then we started talking and the clouds faded long enough for me to see cubicles and those wide filing cabinets. But then Mr. Rios said he was going to show me something, and all the white mist turned green, and I couldn't breathe, and – Alex, maybe we shouldn't be here."

"You want to go home now?"

"Maybe."

"Well, we're here. And I think knowing what might freak out will better prepared you for the future. Whatever happens."

"Alex, I'm scared."

142

"I'd be lying if I said I wasn't. But I really think we should do this. There is, uh, one other thing."

This is it, Samm thought. Maybe now at the steps of A Muse Meant Alex was finally going to tell her what the conversation from the Future-shroom was all about.

"Uh." Alex stammered, clearly uncomfortable.

Samm reached out and placed her hand on his arm. "It's OK, Alex. You can tell me anything. Whatever it is. You're here for me and I'm here for you."

"Yeah, well."

"Anything Alex. It's OK."

"Well, the thing is"

"Yes?"

"The thing is"

"What, Alex? Just say it!"

"I have to go to the bathroom."

Critical Urgency

"Crap, Alex!"

"No, just number one."

"Are you freaking kidding me?"

"No, Samm, I really gotta go."

"I can't believe this. Really?"

"I drank a lot of water with breakfast. Sorry."

Was he kidding her? Were they seriously about
to go into the magic house and meet Mr. Rios just so
Alex could go to the stinking bathroom?

"Don't guys like, go outside and stuff?"

"Really, Samm? I'm hurting over here."

And maybe it was the stress of the whole
situation, or maybe it was a coping mechanism. It
may even have been the unintended humor in
realizing that bathrooms often do stink – bad.
Whatever it was, something struck Samm as funny.
And her whole body started to shake.

"Samm? Are you OK?"

Then the laughter exploded.

"Hey, cut that out."

"I'm not." Samm panted between giggling fits, "Laughing. At you. It's. Just. Funny!"

"I get that, really. But if you laugh, I laugh, and I'm trying to hold it."

Samm got off her bike and turned away from Alex so she could try to get control of her laughter. She tried to focus on any possible entrance from the front of the building. The metal double doors at the top of the steps were chained and locked. Pairs of double hung windows looked in need of washing. The window where they saw Mr. Rios putting out the sign was too high, and they didn't have any ladder or rope appropriate for climbing the building.

"C'mon!" Samm led the way around to the side of the building. Alex guided his bike to the grass, then followed. They both tried pushing up on windows and rattling locked doors. The building took up more space than the empty lot and the diner-filled lot put together. Still, Samm instinctively knew that the building would be even bigger from the inside.

Unlike the metal double doors in front, the doors to the hallways (Samm guessed) were metal framed

145

glass. But the glass was so old and dingy that nothing was visible. Samm could hear Alex whimper a little as he continued to wait for the toilet he needed. His whimper gave her new resolve.

"I'm going to break a window." She told him. "Then, you can reach in and undo the latch."

"Are you sure that's a good idea? Can't you get in trouble for vandalism?"

"This building wasn't here a week ago. But a bathroom might be here today. Besides, I promised your Mom I'd look after you."

Not to mention that Samm was kind of looking forward to the idea. This place felt like a kind of free pass to do things she would never consider at school.

"So, uh, do you want me to help you find a rock or something?"

"Nope. I'm going to kick it. Like a ball sailing past the goalie into nothing but net."

Alex sat next to the window, holding his breath. So many things could go wrong here. Kicking a window was not at all like kicking a soccer ball. Broken glass could cut Samm's foot — or her leg.

She could fall. She could crash into the brick wall.
But he knew better than to stand in her way.

"One act of vandalism, coming right up!"

Samm took several paces back so she could get a
running start. She stared at the wall the way she
would stare down an opponent on the field. Alex
always admired the way she did that. But Alex was
focused on her feet. Because he was, he noticed that
the window broke at least half a second before
Samm's toe made contact with it. The bottom pane
shattered. An excited Samm made a victory lap
around the side of the school, which seemed to
expand just for that purpose and contract as she
returned.

Alex reached in his arm and undid the latch.
Then, he noticed that the room behind the window
was lower than floor level.

"Samm, you're not going to believe this!" He
called.

Samm finished her victory lap and jogged back
to the broken window. "Why not? Could you get it
open?"

"I sure did. But you gotta see this."

"Is it the room I was telling you about?"

"Nope. It's a bathrooom." He paused, letting the information sink in. "The boys' bathroom. The exact thing we needed."

"Well, then, be my guest."

"Do you want me to help you in first? I'll warn you, it's a drop, and I know heights aren't your thing."

"Neither are boys' bathrooms. You do what you need to do, and then you can let me in."

"OK. Just give me a minute."

"Eww! I'm not going to stand here and wait while you pee! I'm going to try to find another way in."

"Suit yourself." Alex reached through the broken window to unlock the latch. Then, when it was unlocked, he pushed up the broken frame so he did not have to maneuver his body around the broken glass.

The boys' bathroom had stalls but no doors. Alex was very glad he only had to pee. He was also glad Samm wasn't in the bathroom with him, or just outside, like she would have been if she hadn't decided to look for another way in. Either would

148

have been weird. But would it have been weird if she hadn't said anything? He was so busy wondering he reached back and flushed the toilet handle without thinking. Then he exited the stall and went to the sink to wash his hands.

He didn't even realize that the toilet flushed — and it shouldn't have — until the water hit his soapy hands. It took the splash of water to make him remember and realize he was in the bathroom of a condemned high school that was supposed to have been demolished and certainly hadn't been there a week ago. He decided his head would hurt if he kept thinking about it, and he really didn't want to, so he turned off the water and was wiping his hands on his pants when he heard Samm scream.

"Coming, Samm!" he yelled.

Not Amused

Alex ran to the hallway where he saw his friend pressing herself against the wall. Between them, a large green reptile with six legs and a bearded dragon's frilled head hissed at her. Four of its legs flailed menacingly as it approached.

"What do I do?" Samm cried.

Alex didn't hesitate. He reached down, pulled off his sneaker, and tossed it down an empty hallway. The creature whirled to the noise, dropped to all six feet like a six-legged alligator, and went to investigate the new noise. Samm slumped in relief.

"That was close." Alex said.

"Too close." Samm agreed. "We need a way out of here. You tossed your shoe the way I came in. Maybe we can leave through the bathroom?"

"We can see. C'mon!" Alex grabbed Samm's hand before she could hesitate, then turned around and retreated back into the boys' bathroom. Samm wrinkled her nose — going into the boys' bathroom still made her uncomfortable — but she followed him.

It didn't matter. The broken window Alex had dropped through was too high.

"You're lucky you didn't break your neck!"

"Maybe if you knelt on my shoulders?" Alex suggested.

"I think I'd have to stand. And then, even if I got through, I couldn't reach down to pull you up behind me.

"You could go and I'd find another way out."

"I don't want us to get separated again. Whatever we do, let's stick together."

"Sure thing."

A few precious moments wasted, they ran out into the hallway again. This time they did not see the creature. Alex ran over and grabbed his shoe. He stuffed his foot back inside and hopped around until both foot and sock were "right."

"Maybe we should try getting out the way I came in?" Samm suggested.

"I thought you wanted to show me A Muse Meant."

151

"And here we are. We've seen it. Let's go home."

"But this just looks like a normal high school."

"Except for the green skinned monster. And the changing, functioning bathroom."

"Well, yeah, except for those things. Still, I wonder where the Goons are. Normally we see them first."

"I'd rather not run into them again."

"Do you think it's safe?"

"No clue."

"Well, what are we waiting for?" Alex forced a brave smile.

"This way." Samm led the pair further down the hallway. Three doors down, she turned left and twisted the knob on the door. Before she or Alex could go through, though, she shut it firmly but softly in front of them.

"What in the world?" Alex asked.

"Goons." Samm said, dropping her voice to a whisper. "In the room. One was halfway out the window. Maybe they're looking for me. I'm almost positive that was the window and this is the room I

came in through. But I don't feel like facing the
Goons. So we've got to find a different way out."

"Whatever you say, Samm."

Samm gave him a dirty look. A fine time to
decide she was in charge. But someone had to be.
She sighed. "We've got to try more doors. Surely one
will lead to a room with a window we can use to
escape. But we have to be quiet."

"You don't have to tell me. What else do you
think we are going to find?"

"Are you trying to invite trouble?" Samm
whisper-shrieked. "I'll open the doors."

"My shoe's at the ready." Alex teased.

"It's still on your foot." Samm pointed out.

"But off in a flash." Alex grinned, attempting to
deflect the situation with some humor.

Samm smiled sarcastically at him. She tried the
second door between the way they had entered and
the boys' bathroom. It was locked. She moved to the
first door.

"Was there a girls' bathroom? Aren't they
normally in pairs – girls and boys?"

"I didn't see one, Samm. But you're right.
Normally they are. Like at the store where they're

separated by the water fountain. Find one and you
find the other. I guess so families stay together,
although that's not such a big thing at a school.
Maybe they wanted to keep the boys and girls
separated here."

"Isn't that odd?"

"I guess we didn't need one."

"This one's locked, too." And there's never been
a girls' bathroom. I washed manure off my hand in
the janitor's closet because I couldn't find a
bathroom. I threw up outside the diner. I wasn't at the
other places long enough.

"Maybe if we thought we needed it."

"We do need a way out and they're all locked –
or blocked by Goons."

"True."

Alex and Samm had come to the end of the
hallway, across from the boys' bathroom. They
turned down the left hallway.

"So it isn't even need based."

"I guess you're right about that. Or maybe we're
supposed to be finding something else."

A MUSE MEANT

In that moment, Samm turned the knob and the door opened. A white-haired man was sitting cross legged on top of a science lab table, scribbling furiously. A small statured figure – the size of a child, but with a beard and wrinkled face like an old man – waited at attention.

"Mr. Rios!" Samm breathed.

If Mr. Rios heard her, he did not acknowledge her. He finished his writing, blew on it, folded it, and gave the folded paper to the other person. "Take this to her in reply. She'll know what's coming. She won't be happy about it, but it's the best I can do for now."

The figure bowed and disappeared.

"Wicked!" Alex breathed.

"And now you two. Hello again, Samantha."

"Samm." Samm and Alex said in unison.

"And you must be Alejandro."

"Alex." The reply from the young people was just shy of a growl.

Mr. Rios was unperturbed by the correction. "I am pleased to meet you of course, but I wish it were under better circumstances. You have disturbed my hexagator and now my Goons have escaped."

"Goons?"

"They left out the window Samm used to enter. Terribly inconvenient, that. But no matter to me. You will be getting them back, I presume."

"You presume?" Alex said. "What are you presuming?"

"You released my Goons. They should not be released. So you will get them back for me."

Samm's dander was up. "And if we don't?"

Mr. Rios removed his spectacles and placed the earpiece thoughtfully under his chin. "You may have noticed that this building did not appear here last week." He stopped for a moment to let that sink in.

Alex gulped. He was pretty sure he knew where this was going.

"And Samantha already observed that she has had access to the entire A Muse Meant complex. That is the ideal configuration, of course. Only a few people ever get to see that. Ever."

Samm's fists clenched at her sides. She knew she would not hit the old man, but losing control over her situation made her angry. She did not know what to do.

156

A MUSE MEANT

"Tonight you knew what you were looking for and you found it. You had what you needed. But you know everything comes with a cost."

Alex and Samm just stared at him. "It is a simple thing. Return my Goons to the basement floor. Give the hexagator back his task. Then you may return home. Fail, and remain. I hope you like cafeteria food. The vending machines have been empty for years."

"Not. Funny." Samm choked through clenched teeth.

"You're absolutely right, Samantha. There is nothing amusing about missing Goons. Their intimidation sucks out imagination – no imagination, no muse."

"My name is Samm." Samm said. "So how do we go about getting your stupid Goons back?"

"Anger to cover fear. Hmmmm. An interesting choice. A fighter's choice." Mr. Rios reflected. "Oh, I do like that. That anger will serve you well if the Goons can't see through it."

Alex was pretty sure the Goons would see right through it. "What are Goons, exactly? How do we find them? How many do we have to get back? What are you going to do when our folks get worried because we haven't come home?"

"Bravo, Alejandro!" Exclaimed Mr. Rios. "You formulated your questions excellently. I can tell you have been paying attention in class. A curious mind is a formidable asset to the endeavor you are about to undertake."

"And does that curiosity get satisfied?" Alex asked. He was scared, but also proud of himself and the five dollar words, as his English teacher would have called them.

"While you are in A Muse Meant, exterior time has no meaning for you. Whether you take four years or four hundred, or four million, when you leave time will resume. But I'm still not sure how much your aging process will be noticed. The outside world is basically unobservant, but in your case…"

"I don't want to be a teenager for four hundred years!"

"Then you better work quickly. Good day." With that, Mr. Rios vanished.

"Wait a minute! You didn't answer my questions!"

158

"He's not going to," Samm said with a sigh. "And that's not even the worst part."

"What could be worse than being a teenager for four hundred years?"

"Alex, you're still twelve." Samm pointed out with a frown. "And I'm only thirteen. Still a tween, technically. We wouldn't even be REAL teenagers for four hundred years."

"Oh, man!"

"C'mon. We can get the Goons back. I did it before. It can't be that hard. We'll just do it again."

"But he didn't tell us anything!"

"Mr. Rios wouldn't give us a job if he didn't think we could handle it. He's a teacher, remember? This is one of those 'learning opportunities' they're always going on about." Samm lifted her fingers to air-quote their teachers' oft-used phrase.

"It's Saturday." Alex grumbled. "Free from learning day." Alex wanted to lift his fingers in a gesture that would show his attitude towards teachers at the moment, but he knew Samm wouldn't appreciate it. Instead, he sighed. "So where do we go from here?"

"Library? It's the best place I can think of to get information."

"Lead the way."

Mrs. Darling Returns

Samm correctly figured that the library would be in the central most part of the school. Her parents had mentioned growing up and coming to the library to hide under tables for tornado drills. Or perhaps the school was being helpful in its own magical ways. In any case, it did not take long for them to find the double doors leading to the precious stacks.

What they did not expect to find was a friendly face.

"Mrs. Darling! What are you doing here?"

"I'm not really here. But you need me. So here I am. That's how this place works."

"Huh?"

"So this place is like a giant Room of Requirement?" Samantha mused.

Mrs. Darling smiled at the Harry Potter reference. "The rules are somewhat different than JK Rowling's, but yes. A Muse Meant is a magical place. Some rooms appear because you wish to find them, but selfish acts or acts of vandalism have consequences. The library will be a place to find useful information, and while I can't tell you everything, I can tell you where to find it."

"So the Goons got out because we broke the window?"

"Exactly."

"But they got out through the window Samm came in, not the one I used to get in. Why didn't they attack me?"

"I'm just special." Samm teased.

"More so than you realize, Samm. I've been trying to tell you."

"Sorry I wasn't paying good enough attention."

"You've had a lot on your mind. But you're here now, and that's what matters."

"And we're stuck here unless we can return the Goons. So how do we get them back?"

"Well, to defeat your enemy, you must first understand him."

"That's like *Ender's Game*, right?"

"Very good, Alex."

"I don't think I could ever love Goons." Alex mused.

"You just have to remember that Goons were – and still are – people." Mrs. Darling said.

"But what about"

"Unh uh. That's the last of my freebies. Research. What can I help you find?"

Samm considered. "Well, we know the Goons are former bullies. And we know that Goons are guarded by the hexagator."

"Good. What else?"

"Goons can be released through acts of selfishness or vandalism." Samm screwed up her face in concentration, trying to think of other things she knew.

"Goons are big and butt ugly." Alex said. Samm and Mrs. Darling glared at him. But then Samm had an idea.

"Goons never grew up! Time stopped for them, but they're just overgrown kids! That's why A Muse Meant is sometimes a magic park – like when I first came without you, Alex. I saw it, but no one else remembers. The Goons need a place to hang out – a place to play and a place to intimidate other people."

"So we've got to build the Goons a Ferris wheel and a roller coaster or something?"

"Or do we just imagine it?" Samm looked at Mrs. Darling.

But instead of Mrs. Darling, Mr. Rios was there. "Excellent work, Samantha. You wasted no time figuring out how to lure the Goons. But now you have to figure out how to unlock A Muse Meant's magic box, so to speak."

"What happened to Mrs. Darling?"

"Isn't it obvious? We figured it out, so technically we don't 'need' her." Samm said. "Except that we still really do."

"Now, now, Samantha," Mr. Rios smiled a slightly ominous half-smile, "one mustn't be selfish. Speaking of which – look over there"

"Look at what? The children turned.

When they turned back, Mr. Rios was gone again.

***

A MUSE MEANT

"I'm hungry." Alex complained. They had been looking at books on Disney World, Worlds of Fun, Universal Studios – any book on amusement parks and how they got started. Anything they could try to use to bring elements of an amusement park to the school. Alex thought if Samm could see the amusement park that she visited, if she imagined Disneyland or Six Flags or something from a picture, perhaps she could recreate it.

Mrs. Darling had not returned.

Samm was fairly certain that the amusement park she had visited with the class was not going to be in some book. The boa constrictor probably violated all sorts of safety codes. The revolving stage likely did, too. She had tried to forget the conversation she'd heard on the Future-shroom when she was there, but it was present in the back of her mind. On top of bringing back the Goons – was Alex ill? Was this cessation of time also a way for Mr. Rios to extend Alex's life? Alex seemed fine to her. But that's the way it went sometimes.

Alex knew something was off with Samm, but couldn't put his finger on what it was. He wanted to stop looking at books and start building something. Or at least he wanted to explore the school more. Where did things in Rooms of Requirement go when they weren't required? If the Room of Requirement held a menagerie, where did the poop go? And he was hungry. He enjoyed books like Samm did, but maybe not as much as Samm did. The sooner they could figure out getting the Goons back, the sooner they could go home. In the meantime, maybe the school had a working cafeteria?

"Hey – do you think this place has a cafeteria or vending machines or something?" Alex asked.

Samm looked at him. "Alex, you know we can't be selfish. We have to figure out a way…"

Alex snapped his fingers. "Cafeterias are great places for bullies! Shaking down kids for their lunch money, tripping kids or hitting their trays so they go flying – food fights?"

Samm admitted that the idea was a good one. She placed a notecard into the travel guide to mark her place, stood up, and dusted herself off. "Lead the way, sir!" she said with forced enthusiasm.

"Yes, ma'am!" Alex retorted with equal force.

166

A MUSE MEANT

They left the library with renewed determination.

***

Even after what must have been decades, the smell of mystery meat lingered over the sheer drabness that was the A Muse Meant cafeteria. Alex was not amused. He had generally believed that high school cafeterias should look the way they did on the Disney Channel. High school cafeterias should be larger than life cool places to hang out. At the very least, they should be large rooms with a second level that might double as a stage for a battle or a hip hop scene, even if they lacked the curtains or anything that would make them really useful for most elementary school cafeteria productions. So while every elementary school cafeteria that Alex could recall had a dedicated stage and curtain, he figured high schoolers had better imaginations and didn't need curtains to hide behind.

But this place was desolate, Alex thought. He was relieved to not be facing a roomful of Goons, but he was disappointed not to see any at all.

"Well, it was worth a shot." Alex said.

Then he noticed Samm. She was gazing intently at a doorway. Then she screamed "look out!" as a laden cafeteria tray came flying through the air at him. He didn't have time to duck. It came out of nowhere. He braced himself for the impact of green Jell-O, mashed potatoes and gravy and Salisbury steak, but when the tray would have touched him, it went through him and disappeared.

"What in the world was that? Did you see that thing? Samm?"

"Here comes another one!"

This time Alex wasn't so lucky. As Samm cried out, the tray took physical shape and this time it did not disappear. Green Jell-O and gravy splattered across Alex's face.

"Gross!"

What Alex could not see, and what Samm could, was the Goon hurling the trays.

"Bad girly! Go away girly!" it cried.

Samm wondered why the Goon was telling her to go away but aiming the trays at Alex. She felt helpless to do more than yell that the trays were coming as they appeared and Alex started trying to dodge what he clearly could not see coming.

"Let's get out of here!" Samm cried when she finally came to her senses.

Covered in cafeteria food, Alex only nodded and they both retreated to the door.

Across from the cafeteria, another boys' bathroom emerged.

"Do you mind?" Alex asked.

"Go ahead." Samm said agreeably. She wondered again why there wasn't a girls' bathroom.

Alex came out a few minutes later. "Hey, why didn't you get hit with anything? And how come you could see it?"

"I'm not sure." Samm replied. "Probably for the same reason that there aren't any girls' bathrooms."

"So, come on. What did you see?"

"Well, there was definitely a Goon launching trays. Didn't you hear him yelling at me to go away? But he was aiming the trays at you."

"He must have realized I couldn't see them – or him. Has that happened before?

"I don't know. You weren't with me during the field trip, but I was the only one who saw more than

169

the lame science center. You've seen Mr. Rios, but I saw him first and I was the one opening the doors. We both saw the hexagator."

"But you saw it first. Weird!" Alex thought for a minute. "Do you remember what that guy said at the library? The scary guy with Mrs. Darling?"

"What guy? Mr, Rios?"

"No, the other one. His friend or whatever. When Mrs. Darling was really Mrs. Darling and not a ghost or whatever. Didn't he say you had special powers?"

Samm didn't want to think about that. She didn't want special powers. She didn't want to be singled out. She didn't want something else that made her different from Alex. She didn't want to be a freak.

Alex saw the look on her face. "Samm, you're not a freak. If you can see things, even if I can't, that's awesome. It will really help us find the Goons so we can get home. The scary guy said you had something special. We need you to use that. I need you to use your gift, Samm."

Alex gently touched the tear that formed on Samm's cheek and lifted it away from her face.

Samm took a deep breath.

170

"OK," she said. "Let's go talk to that Goon."

A Goon Named Greg

Before they went in, Samm described everything she could about the Goon to Alex – where it was, what it looked like, and which way it was facing. Alex didn't know if the Goon would move, rendering him blind once again, but when he reentered the cafeteria with Samm, he could see the Goon just as she had described it. He was standing in the doorway of a cafeteria line with an industrial sized garbage can in front of him and a row of trays sliding on an invisible conveyor belt toward him. Any trays the Goon did not pick up landed squarely in the garbage, which Alex would have thought impossible. The garbage can should overflow at some point. However, as magically as the conveyor transporting the trays, the can remained at the point of just overflowing.

"Bad girly go away." He heard the Goon now, too.

"I can see you, too, now." Alex said. "I won't be so easy to hit."

"Bleh. I don't want your lunch money. You go away, too."

"We aren't going away." Samm said bravely. "We want to bring your friends back here."

"Don't have friends. Go away."

"Do the other Goons pick on you?" Alex asked.

"Nobody is friends. Goons not friends." The Goon insisted.

Samm thought about this. She looked at the Goon. Under the layers of, well, Goony-ness, she could see the outline of a boy. The boy didn't look scary at all. She concentrated on him instead of the Goon.

"Did you have friends before you became a Goon? Do you have a name?"

"Goons not friends. Nobody is friends." The Goon insisted again.

"Well, you weren't always a Goon." Samm insisted right back. The image of the small boy grew brighter. She heard Alex intake a sharp breath beside her, and knew he could see the boy, too. "Once upon

173

a time you were a little boy and you had a name. What happened to you?"

"Goons not friends! Nobody is friends! Bad girly go away!" The Goon cried out, frustrated.

"I'm not going away, and you weren't always a Goon. Talk to me. Maybe we can be friends. Would you like to be friends with me?"

"I wanted this girl named Agate to notice me. Don't you think Agate is a cool name?"

Alex and Samm nodded, urging him to continue.

"Every day I would save Agate a seat at my table. She never noticed. I wanted her to notice me. I wanted her to see I was cool and come sit with me. So I picked up a tray and threw it across the lunchroom, like this." The Goon artfully demonstrated the tray-hurl that had covered Alex not long ago. "Only Agate wasn't there to see it like I thought she was. But other people started clapping. So I picked up another one and threw it. People clapped even more, and said my name. I thought sure Agate would hear the cheering and come."

"Did she come? Did she see you?" Samm asked.

174

"I was throwing trays as hard and fast as I could. People were stomping their feet chanting my name. Then Agate came into the cafeteria." The Goon started to turn away, picked up another tray, and threw it down in front of him in frustration. The contents disappeared.

"I take it she wasn't impressed." Alex said.

"She wasn't looking where she was going." The Goon stammered.

"Oh, no," Samm said. "She fell."

"She blamed you and never forgave you – is that it?" Alex guessed.

"No, Alex." Samm said. "Worse." All of a sudden, Samm saw the cafeteria in her mind. There was a rowdy rabble of students chanting some name. A dark-headed girl, nose in a book, came into the cafeteria. She looked up to see why everyone was chanting.

"She slipped on some Jell-O," Samm said. "Or maybe some gravy. She hit her head really hard on the floor. Did she die?"

"I don't know!" cried the Goon. "I ran away to hide, but Mr. Rios found me. He told me I just had to clean up the trays and then I could go home." The

Goon indicated the scene in front of him. "But the trays just keep coming. I eat them, clean them, throw them – they don't stop coming. I'll never be done."

"How long have you been here?" Alex asked.

"A week? Maybe a month?" The boy/Goon scratched his head.

Samm noticed a poster on the wall. It was a book fair advertisement; a drawing of Harry Potter was the main feature.

"Do you know who that is?" Samm asked the Goon/boy.

"Some magic kid." Said the Goon/boy. "There's a movie about him coming out, I think. He can ride a broom, talk to a snake, and this guy takes off his – his something — and he has another head growing behind his head. Weird."

"We know the movie." Alex said. "There are — ow!"

Samm kicked Alex before he could tell the Goon how many Harry Potter films had been made. Suffice to say more than a decade had passed with the boy doing nothing except cleaning trays. Samm wondered if that was how she and Alex would be. How much time was passing outside the school? If they couldn't find the Goons, would they be replacing them?

And this boy — as Samm now thought of him — this boy wasn't bad or a bully. He'd just made a mistake while trying to get a girl to notice him. In an unfortunate, macabre way, it was sweet.

"As I was saying, there are posters of Harry Potter at our school, too." Alex amended. He looked over at Samm, as if to say "I wasn't going to tell this guy how old he is!" even though Samm was sure that was exactly what Alex would have said had she not kicked him.

"What name were they shouting in the cafeteria?" Samm asked Alex. "Could you make it out?"

"It was one syllable." Alex struggled to remember. "Craig? Grant?"

"Greg," said the Goon/boy. "They were shouting Greg, Greg, Greg." The Goon/boy looked at Samm and Alex. "My name is Greg! My name is Greg!"

"Nice to meet you Greg. I'm Samm."

"I'm Alex."

"I'm Greg. I'm Greg! Pleased to meet you!"

"Pleased to meet you, too."

177

The Goon's outer shell withered and faded. The boy inside was changing, too. Growing, maturing.

Before their eyes, the awkward boy changed into a gangly teenager. Greg's face was a pimpled mess and his hair was greasy enough to be served at a fast food restaurant. Samm could see why Agate might not have been interested in him, especially if he hadn't taken the time to try to get to know her first. But unlike the sullen Goon, this boy's face was calm. He was older and wiser now, despite not having aged past the point he was in high school.

"Hey," Greg said. "Are you guys still in elementary school? What are you doing here?"

He had a tray in his hand, and Samm noticed that the cafeteria was once again full of students. But they weren't chanting Greg's name. They were just talking and eating and goofing around.

"We're on a field trip and we got lost." Samm said quickly. She didn't bother correcting him on what school they went to. "Can you help us find the library?"

"Uh." Greg looked around to see who would see him talking to the little kids. "I guess so."

"Thanks." Samm said.

Greg started to leave the doorway, but an invisible force held him back. "Oh, I forgot. I'm in detention, and have to clean the lunch trays."

Samm said, "They look clean to me. What do you think, Alex?"

Alex looked, and they were – clean and stacked and no longer sliding along the conveyor belt. Samm had broken the spell on them!

"Oh. Wow." Greg said. "I finally finished. I thought I'd be in detention forever."

Samm didn't bother to correct him. Time was shifting in weird ways, and she wanted to ask Mrs. Darling about it.

The trio reached the library doors just as a dark haired girl was coming toward them. "Here you go, guys." Greg said. "Do you need me to come in with you so you can find your teacher?"

The dark-haired girl looked up. "Oh, how sweet! Hi, kids!"

Alex looked up and his heart fluttered a little. "Hi."

Samm was not amused. "Greg, thanks so much for helping us get to the library during your lunch.

We're fine now. You should go before your food gets cold."

Greg might not have been the brightest crayon in the box, but he took Samm's hint. "Yeah, I gotta get back. Agate, can I escort you to the cafeteria? You can tell me about the book you're reading."

Behind Agate, Samm nodded. It might not end in romance or a happy ending at all, but maybe now Greg and Agate had a chance to become friends.

"I'd like that." Agate smiled.

"Right this way, milady." Greg gestured grandly. Agate giggled.

Alex started to make a gagging noise, but Samm pushed him into the library before Greg or Agate could hear.

"So are they going to be boyfriend and girlfriend now?" Alex asked.

"We don't know and it doesn't matter. Greg won't be a Goon anymore, though. I think."

Mr. Rios was perched on a tall stool near the check-out area. One foot rested on the bottom rung. The other hung suspended just above the floor.

"Well done." Mr. Rios said. "Though you didn't manage to secure any food for yourselves." Four peanut-butter-and-jelly sandwiches appeared at the check-out counter, along with two apples and two cartons of milk.

Alex's stomach growled.

"Is it safe?" Samm asked. "Is it like fairy food that will trap us here?"

Mr. Rios chuckled. "I certainly appreciate your active imagination, Samantha."

"That isn't an answer to my question."

"You're right. I suppose you'll just have to trust me. Or not."

Samm looked at Alex.

"I have to eat something. Why don't I be the guinea pig? If something bad happens to me, you can save me. If nothing bad happens, then we can both eat. The cafeteria will be safe now."

Samm was not certain of this logic. The way A Muse Meant changed, it would be very easy for Mr. Rios to put another Goon in Greg's place, or to put Greg back.

"Your house. Your rules." She told the old man. "But it isn't fair to have a game where only one person knows how to win."

"You're absolutely right, Samantha. I'm not being fair." Mr. Rios said agreeably. Then his face turned. "But who told you life was fair? Perhaps you'd rather explain to your parents how you broke a window to break into a school?"

"But the school isn't even here!"

"But you really did break a window. And I can't exactly go to the hardware store and fix it, now can I?"

"Can't you use magic?"

"Kids these days. Always wanting shortcuts. Always wanting easy. Fair." Mr. Rios got off the stool and walked towards Samm. He got right in her face. "Life isn't fair!" he shouted. "Life isn't easy," he said in a quiet voice that was more terrifying than his shout, "and life is not about shortcuts. Why else haven't I crossed over? Why am I still here? Do you think I want to be?"

A MUSE MEANT

Samm hadn't considered that. What was a retired teacher doing corralling bullies in a magical school, anyway?

"You don't know all the rules, either. Do you?" Samm asked as gently as she could.

Mr. Rios turned away from her, and wouldn't answer. Samm didn't think he had to.

Finally, he spoke. "The food is safe. Eat — and be strong. You have a long night ahead of you both. Use whatever means you can. Find my Goons and bring them back."

Then he walked through the stool, through the check-out desk, and through a closed door marked AV room.

"Wicked." Alex walked over to the sandwiches. "Hey, mine are strawberry jelly. Yours are apple. He knows our favorites."

Samm joined Alex. It was breaking the rules to have food in the library, but she was hungry. She picked up one of the sandwiches and opened it. The peanut-butter-and-jelly were a perfect consistency. She took an experimental bite. It was really good. But now that she knew Mr. Rios wasn't making all the rules, she had a jumbled new list of questions and no true idea where to start. She mulled over the problem between bites. She chewed each one slowly and thoughtfully. Alex, on the other hand, was wolfing down the food like he hadn't eaten in days.

And maybe he hasn't. Samm thought to herself. Maybe we haven't. He trusts me to figure a way out of this mess. I'm still a kid, too, though.

Defeating Paradox

"Maybe if we raided the art department and got a whole bunch of paint and stuff, they'd want to come back so they could graffiti the place."

"Maybe."

"Or maybe we could raid the teacher's lounge for drugs and alcohol." Alex suggested next.

"Really?" Samm raised an eyebrow. "Drugs and alcohol?"

"Why not?" The teachers have to keep it somewhere after they take it. And you know there's always been that rumor about that one history teacher…"

"If they take stuff, it's supposed to go to the office."

"OK, then we raid the office!"

"Probably they've already done that. We've got to give them something they really want."

"We did. Freedom."

"Something more than that. If it were just about dodging authority, they would have been skippers, not bullies. They want – they need – to be in charge, to lord over other people. They want…"

"Mr. Rios on a plate."

"Exactly."

"But that's never going to happen."

"Why not?"

"He'll never go for it."

"So you keep saying. But why do you think he wouldn't."

"Would you? They're Goons, for crying out loud."

"True, but I'm not a teacher. Besides. He already did, once."

"What?"

"It's the paradox. Mr. Rios died at the hands of some of these bullies. To keep them here, he has to keep dying."

"That's awful."

"Which is why we have to talk him into it."

"No way."

"We have to"

"Forget it. No way am I going to tell some teacher he has to get bullied to death."

"He's already dead."

"Exactly."

"And we don't have a choice. We have to get out of here, and Mr. Rios said the only way to make that happen is by making the Goons return. The only way to make the Goons return is to give them Mr. Rios. They aren't going to settle for anything less."

"They could bully us."

"Yeah, but we're just kids. We don't pose a threat. We aren't authority figures."

"Well, you can be kinda bossy."

"Shut up."

"Yes, ma'am."

"Alex, c'mon! Get serious. Don't you want to go home?"

"Yeah."

"Then we need to talk to Mrs. Darling again. C'mon."

***

They walked back to the circulation desk and pressed the buzzer. Mrs. Darling materialized.

"How can I help you?"

"We need Mr. Rios to agree to something."

"Yeah, and he's not going to like it."

Mrs. Darling frowned. She fidgeted with her hair and pressed her hands down the front of her pants as though she could iron out wrinkles that way.

"What do you need from him?"

"Well, we have to give the Goons something they want in order for them to come back."

"And we figured that the only thing they want is him."

"Who figured?" Mrs. Darling asked.

"Samm did. But she's right. She's figured it out.

"Yes, yes she has." All heads spun to see Mr. Rios' XYZ figure walking toward them from the periodicals section. "But even if I were to be your sacrificial lamb, how would my Goons know you caught me."

Samm had thought about this, too. "We're going to take part of Alex's idea about raiding the art room and graffiti-ing the outside of the building. Then

188

we're going to raid the TV room and broadcast our vandalism to every TV and internet station we can find. Kids will share our prank with other kids, and that information will get back to the Goons, who will come looking for us and you."

"And how are you going to get me to agree."

"The paradox. You already did."

Mr. Rios feigned surprise. "I did what?"

"These Goons killed you once before. You died defending what you loved. The paradox says you have to do it again."

"You're awfully sure of yourself."

"You're a good teacher."

"Hmm." Mr. Rios stuck his hands in his pockets and sauntered away. Alex was about to follow him, tackle him if he had to, but Samm put her hand on his chest to stop him. Mr. Rios walked about 10 steps, turned, and then just stopped, as if lost in thought. Samm assumed he was.

Then he amazed her still further by pulling a book off the shelf. "Here," he said, handing it to her, "This was in the wrong place."

Samm looked down. A copy of *The Lion, the Witch, and the Wardrobe* was in her hand. Like

189

magic, she put her thumb on an interior page and opened up to see the mighty Aslan tied to the great stone table. She looked up at Mr. Rios, a tear threatening to give her away.

"Oh, don't look at me like that." Mr. Rios turned away from her again and started to walk away. "I'm hardly blameless or sinless. I'm just a man – or I was, once."

Samm wasn't sure how to respond to that, so she didn't. She waited.

"You might even say less than a man." From across the room, he turned back to her. "Haven't I bullied you? Don't you deserve to get back at me?"

"Yes!" Alex said, uncertain as to why.

"No!" Samm said. "It's not like that. It's just…"

"You want to go home." Mr. Rios said. "It's all right. It isn't selfish. You are so young. You have so much life ahead of you."

"Yes." Samm choked.

"You are right about the paradox, young Samantha. Truth be told, I hadn't thought about it in years. But that doesn't make it invalid."

"So why give me the book? This book?"

"It was misshelved."

"You knew it was there."

"I've already agreed to be your sacrifice – what more do you want from me?" Mr. Rios dragged his hands through his hair as his suspenders heaved with the weight on his shoulders. All of the sudden, he looked every bit of his advanced age – and broken.

"I'm just following the clues you give me!" protested Samm.

"You are creating the game, girl! All of this is on you."

"All of this?"

"Your game. Your stories. Your rules. You hold all the cards here, madame, and once you realize that – once you realize the powers and responsibilities you have…"

"I become you?"

"No." Mr. Rios sighed heavily. He smoothed his hair with his hands, something that could only have been accomplished with decades of practice, slid his thumbs down his suspenders, adjusted his bow tie, and took deep breaths to steady himself. When Samm thought he must have finished his ritual of calming and passed his self-inspection, he walked back to Samm.

"This is your world, Samantha. I am a piece of your chessboard. A powerful piece, but just a piece. You decide where I go."

"Why me?"

"Why not you? Since the very first time you walked into A Muse Meant, you saw it for its possibilities."

To Samm, that field trip was ages ago. She barely remembered all the cool things she saw. She did remember the dangers.

"It was so scary! Alex was leaving. The boas and the goons and the broken ladder."

"I was leaving – what?"

"Ah – you never told Alejandro. Why didn't you?"

"I wanted to change the future. Your world – it couldn't be real. I didn't want your world to be real."

"Especially when he got sick."

"Yeah. Because it could have been like that. It could have been worse."

"Samm, you're scaring me. What on earth are you talking about?"

"Amazing how that affected you more than the boas."

"The boas were plenty creepy."

"Hey! Is anybody going to tell me what the heck's going on?"

"He's right, Samantha. I think you should show him."

"But the Goons."

"I would like one more night before I surrender myself. I would not mind spending it as Ring Master of your peculiar circus."

"Will you be there, too?" Samm asked Mrs. Darling.

"Of course, my dear." The librarian's eyes were kind. Mr. Rios tells me this is better than even he ever dreamed.

"So where should I begin?"

"Why not return to the menagerie in the gymnasium. Save the Future-shroom for last, I should think. It would be good for Alejandro to see what you can do."

"Alright." She turned to Alex finally. "Alex, do you remember how this whole thing got started? We were looking for the abandoned lot, or we were looking for the lame science center you saw online?"

No Ordinary Animals

The next thing she knew, Samm was running breathlessly down the hall, searching for the gymnasium. Alex, confused, was dogged on her heels. "Samm, why can't you just tell me what's going on?"

"I didn't want you to think I had gone *loco*. And trust me, when we didn't find this place, I was worried for myself."

"You know you can tell me anything. You know I'll always believe you."

"I met the Goons before. In this place. They don't like me."

"Yeah – that one day with the ice cream vendor at the diner. That was so weird."

"Yes, but even before that. The day of the field trip. And the day I woke up in the library. Everyone else had a buddy. We came here. But it wasn't like this. It was…"

They had reached the double doors. Samm wondered if they were the right ones. The school was so big.

"Push." Samm told Alex.

"Woah!" Alex breathed in amazement.

Marching around the turnstile now were no ordinary animals. A unicorn, a Pegasus, and of course, two hexagators on hind legs walking upright turned the stages in their lazy pattern.

Instead of students jumping from upper platform to lower, acrobats and circus performers, ribbon climbers and tight rope walkers danced and spun and flew effortlessly in an elaborate dance. Every inch of the stage was a spectacle. There was a giant clown with a huge red nose riding an oversized tricycle with a little clown dog in the basket. Next to the clown, six ladies danced the can-can in teal dresses like Vegas showgirls. Their makeup was dark and heavy, reds and blues in exaggerated fashion. The result was not beautiful, but it was eye-catching. Alex felt like he had gotten on a roller coaster after eating one unfortunate funnel cake too many.

196

"Are you doing this?" He asked Samm.

"This is more. This is different." Samm said. It was everything she could imagine being in a circus. There was the elephant trainer with the tiny perch for the pachyderm. The entertainers were so close together Samm just knew something or someone would get loose, get hurt. And still her mind exploded with circus possibilities. In her hands appeared cotton candy and popcorn. She shut her eyes but the ideas continued, assaulting her, battering her.

"Hey," Alex said. "Is that Mr. Rios with the lion?"

Samm opened her eyes then and saw it was true. Mr. Rios, in a white ruffled shirt with rolled up sleeves, black suspenders, black military dress pants, and a tall black top hat held up a coiled bullwhip in one hand. In the other, he had raised a chair. The lion seemed more bored than ferocious – and certainly could have attacked any number of nature prey on the stage. The other performers did not seem the least bit put out by the lion's presence.

197

"It's just illusions." She whispered, testing to see if the words held true. They were illusions, but solid enough for Alex to see them, too.

"No wonder you wanted me to find this place, Samm." He said. "It's incredible.

"It's not real."

"It's real enough. Come on, let's say hello to Mr. Rios and his cowardly lion."

"No, Alex!"

Samm's panicky thoughts were the lion's deeds. That harmless cat of a moment ago turned on Alex as he approached, and to Samm's horror, picked up speed. She slammed her eyes closed as the lion clamped a screaming Alex by the middle into its massive jaws. In her mind's eye, Samm saw the lion turn with Alex in its mouth like a dog bringing a large doll back to its master.

Her cotton candy and popcorn instantly became a sword and buckler. She ran toward the lion with its back to her. She knew full well it was too late for Alex. She was making too much noise it was probably too late for her. The lion was going to turn around and she would be the next victim and meal.

198

A MUSE MEANT

Then Mr. Rios was there, an arm across her shoulders. Alex was on the floor with a lion slobber soaked shirt, but he was unharmed. Yet how could Mr. Rios be with her? He was still holding the whip and chair on the other side of the theater. And there he was in the group of can-can ladies. And there was his face on the upright hexagator. Samm felt faint.

"I assure you; your friend is quite safe." Mr. Rios said. "You really can't imagine your life without him, so he can never really be gone. Do you understand that? This place cannot take him from you."

Samm could not answer. She was very near hysterical with grief and relief. So many emotions clouded the examination of any single one.

"He's unharmed, Samantha. Open your eyes and look at what you've done."

Samm opened her eyes. She was now above the scene, looking down. Alex lay quite still, on the ground, covered in rich red blood, unmoving. The lion's nose was at Alex's shirt, nuzzling the boy in doglike fashion.

"Hey – that's cold!" Alex said, laughing and sitting up.

As if on cue, the lion put its head down on its front paws. The back legs were still extended, so that the rear end and tail were in the air.

Alex scooped up a handful of the blood-like substance and tasted it. "It's ketchup!" He laughed.

"This isn't real, either." Samm said.

"What is real?" Mr. Rios replied. "If you believe it; if he does. You still don't accept what I tell you as true. This is for your muse meant, which means it is meant for you."

Samm turned and looked at the ring master. He was a teacher. She couldn't forget that. He was just a teacher. Running a circus was his dream. She knew that because Mrs. Darling talked about it.

"Moira. Moira Darling. That's a Peter Pan reference. Is anything real?"

"Who said anything was real? Who said life is real? Samantha, you have read my obituary. I should be resting in peace, or at least be a ghost to you. You are creating this beautiful chaos. Accept the gift. Embrace it. Throw off what you ought to know and just accept what is in front of your eyes."

"But how can you say that?"

A MUSE MEANT

"Does it matter, Samantha? It's OK that this is my life and tomorrow this will all be just a dream to you. Is it OK that I don't want to be remembered by you as a bad dream?"

Big tears started to roll down Samm's face. "I never wanted to hurt you."

"And you haven't, child. You have helped me fulfil a dream. Look at me over there."

They looked. There was Mr. Rios. Bowing to an enthusiastic crowd. He had a red coat and black breeches and tall black books and held his top hat over his heart in an amazing flourish.

They looked again. There was Mr. Rios. In a white open collared tunic, chair in one hand, whip in the other, the lion fierce, threatening, and totally under his control.

They looked again. There was Mr. Rios, appropriately dressed in a tuxedo this time, smiling and surrounded by gorgeous ladies all dancing the can-can in unison.

They looked again, and Mr. Rios was in the stands selling peanuts, his rough white shirt rolled up at the sleeves, black suspenders blending with the vendor's box and the cord around his neck. This Mr.

Rios looked tired and hot but obviously took pride in his work. The Mr. Rios next to Samm squeezed her shoulder.

"Thank you."

"What did I do?"

"You see all of me."

Goon Trap

The couches in the teacher's lounge made good sleeping spots for Samm and Alex. After many hours of spectacle, Samm just couldn't keep her eyes open any more.

The next morning, they laid out a plan for what had to be done to attract and trap the Goons.

"Spray paint."

"Video equipment."

"Rope."

"WiFi."

"Don't we need to fix the window so they can't get out again?"

"Samantha, do you need the window to be broken?" Mr. Rios asked. His voice was light, and held the hint of laughter.

"I don't know, Mr. Rios," Samm replied saucily. "Do I?"

"I don't believe you do."

"Then I don't either."

Alejandro, it appears that Samantha no longer has need of a broken window."

"OK. Then should we fix it?"

"No. If she doesn't need it to be broken, then it isn't."

"This is just too weird." Alex exclaimed. At the same time, he still knew something was niggling at the back of his mind. He saw a great number of fantastic things. But he didn't see the Boa Coaster or the mushroom land he'd heard Samm and Mr. Rios talking about. He was trying to decide if it bothered him. But after being grabbed by the playful lion, and thinking he was a goner, he had been distracted last night. It had been fun...

"Earth to Alex." Samm teased. Then, more seriously, she asked. "Alex, are you OK?"

"Yeah, I was just thinking about last night."

"That was something, wasn't it?"

"Yeah. It sure was."

"When that lion got you, I thought you were dead."

Alex laughed. "Believe me. So did I!"

A MUSE MEANT

Samm saw the questions in his eyes. She knew the Future-shroom was on the other side of the doors to the stage, and not the ones they used. If she would even imagine it the same way twice. She really wasn't sure. And she knew there would be plenty of time to talk to Alex after. Lots of things could wait in light of Mr. Rios' sacrifice. His last hours should be about that. They should focus on him.

"We should both focus on Mr. Rios." Alex and Samm said together. Then they laughed again.

"Jinx!"

"Double Jinx!"

"Triple Jinx!"

"Padlock!"

It felt good to laugh and to be so in sync. Even if it was just for one more miserable perfect day. One day that, outside A Muse Meant, would not even exist at all.

***

Samm felt quite naughty spraying cans of paint on the brick walls of the school. She was in the courtyard.

Alex was inside connecting with schools make making sure the video of the vandalism would be seen anywhere the Goons could have gotten. How far could a Goon travel in a day, anyway? Could they travel as far as Samm could think about them traveling? Maybe he shouldn't mention that thought to Samm. He didn't want to be hijacking feeds all over the world. Of course, it might be funny. Like something you see when aliens take over the world on Doctor Who. Focus. He had to focus or he was never going to be ready in time.

As if on cue, Mr. Rios appeared. "How goes your progress, young Alejandro?"

"Not too bad. Not too bad. Listen, I was thinking…"

"Yes?"

"And I don't want to say anything to Samm because anything she thinks of here can happen, and so I don't want her thinking the worst of anything, right?"

"That sounds reasonable."

"But can I ask you something? And then, if you think it's a good idea, run it past her?"

"I think that would be acceptable. Perhaps it would even be wise. What do you have in mind, young man?"

"Well, I was thinking about what you said about the window we broke. About how it didn't need to be fixed when Samm didn't need it to be broken?"

Mr. Rios' eyes lit up. He loved it when his students were thinking independently, no matter what the result.

"Go on." He said.

"And I was thinking about your circus yesterday and how she pictured you in so many different places at once doing so many different things?"

Mr. Rios nodded at Alex to continue.

"So I was thinking that if Samm thought about it, the Goons could be anywhere."

"I can see why you wouldn't want to share that thought with Samantha."

"Well, yeah. But isn't the opposite true as well? If Samm requires all the Goons to be here, wouldn't they have to come?"

Mr. Rios nearly danced a jig. "Well done, my boy. Well done, indeed. That is stellar thinking."

207

"So why are we doing any of this? Why don't we just tell Samm she can think the Goons back?"

"Because Samantha can't do that."

"But you just said she could."

"It is true that this is Samantha's world and Samantha makes the rules for it. However, Samantha believes that magic must be paid for. She believes the Goons require me as a sacrifice. So I extracted a magical night from her."

"But you won't be tortured forever?"

"I hope a stasis point will be reached."

"You hope? Don't you know?"

"No, Alejandro. I really don't. I told you. I," he drew out the syllable, emphasizing it and waggling his eyes at Alex, "don't make the rules here. Young Samantha does."

"That's got to be awful for you, sir."

"It's alright, Alejandro. I have faith in our Samantha. "

"Is she ever going to tell me about that other thing?"

"I wouldn't press her too hard about it, if I were you."

"But, like, do I have anything to worry about?"

"I should think so. You're trying to attract a bunch of escaped Goons here and if you don't manage to bring that danger to your front door then you'll stay here forever in suspended time. Isn't that plenty to worry about?"

"Gee. Thanks for the perspective." Alex rolled his eyes.

"Of course, Alejandro," said Mr. Rios. But whether he was being sincere, ironic, or clueless, Alex couldn't tell.

Alex worked in amicable silence while Mr. Rios observed. Finally, twelve lights that had been flashing orange switched to blue, and the back of Samm's head and shoulders filled the viewscreen.

Alex scoffed a little at her poetry, but overall liked the spray painted effect of the message. He hoped the Goons could not resist a dare. He hoped that Goons could read.

"We have Mr. Rios.
We will share
Meet us in the courtyard.
If you dare!"

Then Alex had panned down to the chair where Samm was trying Mr. Rios. He would have preferred that she acted like she was having fun – laughing and smiling as she tied him up. But Samm couldn't. Of course she couldn't. They hoped her grim determination was compelling enough to convince the Goons.

If the Goons could read, they would know they had been dared. Here's hoping that Samm wanted Goons that could read and could not ignore a dare. In the meantime, they'd wait.

***

But Goons did not arrive that day. After painting her message daring Goons to come get Mr. Rios, Samm tagged the wall until she ran out of spray paint. Though honestly, it didn't take long to run out of paint. Alex made video of Mr. Rios tied up in the courtyard, Samm painting, and the message into a video. He set the video on a loop, making sure the message was visible for 30 seconds every two minutes. Then he and Mr. Rios returned to Samm. Well, Alex walked back to the courtyard. Mr. Rios disappeared and then reappeared.

Samm set down the paint cans. "Is it enough?"

"It looks good, Samm."

"Positively expulsion-worthy, Samantha. Well done."

Samm beamed.

"You really think so? I know I'm not much of an artist."

"I do. If it looked too artsy, the Goons might realize it's a set-up."

"I hope you're right. How long do you think it will take for them to show up?"

"See it, Samantha – and tell us."

Samm thought about all the epic battles she'd read. And since time meant nothing here, they could take the time they needed to prepare – the rest of their lives, if they wanted.

She looked at Mr. Rios. She considered the many sacrifices he'd made for his students and the one he was still offering to make.

211

When it was all over and they went home, would she even remember? Would Mrs. Darling and her friend play with her memory again? Would she be able to trust what she thought anymore?

She looked at Alex, whose eyes had not left her face. He had such faith in her. She would protect him. She would be worthy of his opinion of her. Time may not be passing in the outside world, for their parents, or for anyone else, but they had already spent two days in A Muse Meant and there wasn't any point in waiting longer.

She understood that there probably wasn't going to be much of a battle. Her side was doing all the giving – and only wanted one thing in return. The only way for them to lose was if the Goons did not return.

She just had one question left. "Mr. Rios, what time is the tardy bell?"

"Time really has no meaning here. It could be any time you wanted it to be."

"I know we can go to any time. But there have to be rules to follow so the Goons have rules to break."

"That makes sense. The tardy bell rings at 8:15 each morning. However, that's as frequent or as infrequent as necessary."

"Eight fifteen works for me" Samm said. "They'll want to be late so they can be a disruption. They wouldn't come to the school after dark – they'd have better things to do than school then. They won't come early for the same reason."

"Ok." Alex replied. "So you've figured out the time. Do you know what day?"

"Tomorrow. It's the third day. They're coming tomorrow.

"Then we better be ready."

Big Goon Battle

"Ok. Great. Tomorrow's the big epic Goon Battle. But what will we actually do when they get here?"

"They'll take Mr. Rios, and then they'll go back to the basement."

"Yeah, for how long?"

"Alex – that's not fair! You know how hard this is for me. But Mr. Rios agreed to be the sacrifice, and magic has a price!"

Samm looked to Mr. Rios for support.

"I am your sacrifice. I've exacted my price. It would be unwise of me to attempt renegotiation of terms at this point."

"You can't RE negotiate what you never negotiated in the first place, sir!" Alex said. "The Goons serve you in Muse Meant to pay for their past deeds. If they can change, they go back to being humans in their own time. We saw that with Greg. If they can't change, I'm not sure how it happens outside of time, but they become hexagators. They don't stay Goons forever, so we aren't going to let you be their prisoner forever. There has to be another way." Alex looked so pointedly at Samm that she started to cry.

"What do you want from me, Alex?"

"Tell us that Mr. Rios is going to be OK. See it, Samm. See it and fix it. We've got all the time in the world to get it right, so there's no need to rush into things."

"Then you tell me how to fix it, Alex. I don't know."

"You know I can't, Samm. This is your world. This is your magic. You're just going to have to figure it out on your own."

"I need to go to the library!"

"No need, dear. I'm here."

Samm didn't care whether Mrs. Darling was real, a ghost, a robot, or a hologram. And she didn't care. She ran to Mrs. Darling and hugged her hard.

Mrs. Darling hugged her back and smoothed her hair. Finally, Samm broke away. Her face was splotched and red.

"Alex thinks I can save Mr. Rios."

"What do you think?"

"I want to."

"I believe you."

"I'm just not sure I can."

"I know."

"Alex and Mr. Rios keep saying this is my world, and my magic."

"Yes, they do."

"But how can it be when I don't know about it? How can I be in control when I feel so out of control?"

"Obviously they believe in you. Do you believe in yourself?"

Samm didn't have a reply. She thought she had good self-esteem, because she knew she wasn't like those girls who ignored her and giggled at Alex and the other boys. She preferred her books, her thoughts, and her ideas. She didn't know if that made her independent and self-assured or if she was just fooling herself.

"I need time to think." Samm said. Mrs. Darling, Mr. Rios, and Alex disappeared behind a mist.

"Weird." Samm said.

A MUSE MEANT

Because she thought better with pencil and paper in hand, she imagined she had them. They appeared. Just for fun, she imagined a large pink elephant. It appeared and trumpeted around the room, shaking the room so hard Samm was dumped to the floor. She shrunk the elephant to puppy size and imagined a fence for it to run around in. She imagined the fence filled with fresh sweet hay. The elephant stopped frolicking and put its trunk down to the hay. Samm enlarged it to small phony size. It would go into the menagerie when this was over. She imagined another elephant – a small one made out of rose quartz. It appeared in her hand, with a silver chain. Samm put the necklace on, and fingered the tiny elephant.

"I do believe." She smiled.

She wrote nothing on the paper – she didn't need to now. She dismissed it and the mist and the others reappeared.

"Alex is right. And it's 8:10. Everyone needs to get into place."

"But what's the plan?" Alex asked.

"I don't have time to explain." Samm said, fingering her elephant. She'd already imagined the larger one to find its way to the menagerie. "You're going to have to trust me."

Alex nodded, but looked scared.

"Mr. Rios, I'm very sorry about this, but it's time." Samm lifted her head slightly, and stifled a giggle as Mr. Rios flew backward into a high backed chair, ropes flying around to secure him into place. She had to work quickly. She could feel the Goons approaching.

"Mrs. Darling, take Alex to the library. It won't be safe for him, and I don't want him to see this."

"C'mon Alex."

"No! Samm – you haven't solved anything! You're just ignoring the problem! Like you've been doing to me ever since the stupid field trip!"

"I'm sorry, Alex. I need the Goons to win right now. This is the best way."

Samm touched her little pink elephant, then dropped down to one knee. Goons appeared from every direction. They swarmed Mr. Rios so thickly that the man could not be seen except for the occasional glimpse of fluffy white hair.

"Samm! How could you just give up? Samm!"

A MUSE MEANT

Samm looked up and looked at Alex. Her words would only be a whisper, but he would have to hear her and believe it. "I thought you trusted me, Alex."

The Goons emitted a joyous cacophony. Friends turning against each other was a hallmark of bully success. Always one would try to stand up for themselves or the group. The group would abandon the victim – sometimes the weakest, sometimes the strongest — to save themselves. Then it was simple to divide and conquer the rest.

Meanwhile, Samm waited for what she expected her friend to say. She could have made him say it. She knew that now. This was her world. But even in her world, people had to make their own choices. If she allowed the Goons that much, how could she deny her best friend?

Alex looked absolutely defeated. Mrs. Darling had an arm around him to usher him away. And for 10 heartbeats, he let her. Then he turned around.

Samm had only seen Alex with tears in his eyes a couple of times in her life. This one would be seared into her memory. He looked at her, looked at Mr. Rios through his attackers, and looked at her again.

"Samm, I thought this was your world. Not theirs. Don't let the bullies win."

"You thought this was my world?" Samm said softly.

"I did."

"What a coincidence. I do, too." Samm smiled as she walked confidently through the throng of Goons. They parted for her like water, frozen in suspended time. She reached Mr. Rios' chair and kissed the top of his head. "Thank you, Mr. Rios, for your sacrifice."

First, his ropes fell away. Next, the high-backed chair to which Mr. Rios had been tied transformed into a Ferris wheel bucket seat complete with plush leather padding and the bar that snapped across the surprised teacher. The seat lurched backward, then up into the air. The Goons had to scatter as their prey shot up into the air over their heads on a Ferris wheel that was being constructed right before their eyes.

Mr. Rios looked at her, eyes wide with fear. He looked like he wanted his ropes back.

Samm giggled. She guessed Mr. Rios was as terrified of heights as she was; allowing himself to be tossed around was an added element to his sacrifice. The bottom of the Ferris wheel rose level with the roofline of A Muse Meant. When it stopped, Mr. Rios, occupying the only seat on the wheel, was stuck at the very top.

Some Goons would not be deterred. They started to climb the A-frame of the Ferris wheel, determined to capture their prize. Samm let them get halfway. Then, she brought the rain.

While Mr. Rios undoubtedly shivered and froze at the top of the Ferris wheel, a torrential downpour washed the Goons away like so many waterspout spiders.

Samm was so cold – despite her excitement at how well her plan was working. She looked across the courtyard at Alex. He was grinning and shivering. They'd probably both be in bed with pneumonia after this – on top of being grounded. Served Alex right for not going to the library with Mrs. Darling like she'd tried to get him to do. But in that moment, the idea of being sick and grounded, compared to everything else they'd faced, sounded really good. Moreover, Samm knew that facing the consequences of her actions was a sacrifice she could make to pay for the magic. Mr. Rios' confinement would haunt her until it was over. She could never be free until he was – until they all were.

"We are all free to make our own choices, Goons." Samm shouted through the storm. Magically, her voice carried. And she was still heard even though she delivered her next line in a whisper. "We are not free from the consequences of our choices."

She'd never really understood that before. Now she did. Mr. Rios never controlled the Goons. She wouldn't either – how could either of them? Goons were people – students like her – once. Either they would serve their time, forgive themselves, and move on, or they would fall victim to something else.

The rain beat down in driving sheets. It prickled Samm's skin but she nearly didn't notice. Instead, she was watching the top Goons on the Ferris wheel. They were slipping and sliding, and nowhere near the top, but they were also changing. Overalls were washing away, being replaced with gym shorts and faded tees, blue jeans, stiff polo collars and chinos, pocket protectors, cheerleading outfits and football jerseys, even stiff private school uniforms Samm knew the school tried one year to reduce bullying. Every clique or anti-clique was represented. Clean green-tinged skin became any shade of brown – from the palest white to the darkest black. The young people emerging from their grotesque Goon skins were grinning from ear to ear – just like Greg had. But not all the Goons were changing for the better.

Near the poles of the giant Ferris wheel, some Goons writhed in pain. Extra appendages sprang from the armpits of their overalls, which fell away to reveal an alligator's body.

Samm didn't hesitate. She opened the sewers underneath the school. The newly minted hexagators made a hasty retreat from the rain to the sewers below.

With the hexagators gone, the young people, most of whom clung to the horizontal bars that gave support to the A-frames of the Ferris wheel, started to slide down the legs and walked freely into clouds of nothingness. Samm hoped they were going back to their own times. She saw a lifetime of second chances.

223

Pink Elephants

When the rain stopped, Samm sank to the ground.
She pulled her knees up to her chest, and for reasons
should could not articulate, burst into tears. She cried
for the hexagators who condemned themselves to the
sewers. She cried for Mr. Rios. She cried for Alex
and for herself, and for all the times she'd wanted to
cry and didn't.

Alex escaped from Mrs. Darling's grasp.
"Samm, that was amazing! What did you do? What's
wrong?"

"They have a choice now – the Goons, that is.
The hexagators chose the sewers. A lot of Goons
chose forgiveness and to return to life. There are
ways to escape the school." Samm sniffed and looked
up at Alex. "But for Mr. Rios to have his freedom
someday, I have to sacrifice ours."

"So we're stuck here forever?"

"No. We can go home. Speaking of – goodbye, Mrs. Darling. See you at school Monday."

"Goodbye Samm. You did great. I'm so proud of you." Then Mrs. Darling dissipated.

"You get a choice, too, Alex. I brought you here to show you a magical mushroom."

"Cool. I didn't know you were into that, but."

"Not like that." Samm knew Alex was teasing, but what he needed to hear her say was more important. "I heard us talking when we were older. You were leaving. You were telling me to move on. Without you."

"Why did I say that?"

"I have no idea. At first I thought you were horribly sick with some disease or something. Then I thought maybe you were being deported."

"Deported? Samm, I'm Puerto Rican."

"I know, I know. It was silly. And I thought maybe your dad's job or – well, I had a lot of time to think about a thousand and one possibilities ranging from slightly problematic to absolutely terrifying."

Alex started to speak, but Samm stopped him.

"Please, let me finish. I was so worried about you leaving that I pushed you away. I didn't mean to.

225

But I'd never had to think before about whether or not I could stand on my own two feet."

"But nobody does that, Samm. Everybody has people they love that they count on. King Arthur told his knights to defend the weak. When he appeared weak, they defended him."

"I know." Samm fingered her pendant again.

"Hey, is that new? What is that?"

Samm held up the tiny pink elephant so he could see it. She giggled. "It's an elephant."

"It's cool. Have you always had that?"

"Nope. I just made it actually. There's a pony-sized version in the menagerie now – but it's not made of quartz."

"So – why?"

"To remind me not to ignore the elephant in the room."

Alex groaned and wrinkled his nose. They both laughed. "Geez, that's bad, Samm."

"You should have seen it elephant-sized!"

"You mean — you're not going to show me?"

"C'mon, I'll show you the pony-sized one in the menagerie."

"Cool. Much better than mushrooms."

"Excuse me. Samm, Alex? Would you mind ever so much allowing me to rejoin you on firm ground?"

"Oops." Samm said. "I didn't mean to leave him up there." Samm looked over at the Ferris wheel. She imagined it melting into fluffy marshmallow goo. Mr. Rios descended gracefully as if he was riding a remote-controlled cloud. Still, when his feet touched the ground, and he stood up, his legs were shaky. Alex ran to his side to help him.

"Thank you, Alejandro. It'll just take me a minute to get my land legs back."

"Are you OK?" Samm asked him.

"Never better, dear girl. You did very well. I can take it from here."

"I know you could, but you don't have to. You can choose, too."

"I have chosen, dear Samantha." Mr. Rios looked almost embarrassed, but it could have just been his soaking wet state. "I will always be here to guide those that need me."

He held out an arm to her, and Samm ran into it and hugged him.

227

***

Later, Alex remembered Samm telling him that he had a choice, before her confession about hearing their future. "So what choice do I have, Samm?"

"Any choice. Every choice. Not all the Goons became hexagators or cured during the storm. Some of the Goons are choosing to stay and take care of the animals. They don't want to go back to their time. Some are trying to escape. When they do, they're going to find way to do it. By making Goons aware that they have choices here, I'm taking away a lot of what it means to be a Goon to them."

"Well, who'd want to be a Goon anyway?"

"Why would anyone choose to play football – or be a cheerleader?"

They both shuddered. But they knew classmates who aspired to these things.

"I don't know. I only know that they get to choose, and I may think they choose wrong every time, but someone has to be there. To protect people they might hurt and to keep reminding them that they have a choice."

"So that's where we come in."

"Only if you choose it – and only for as long as you choose it."

No Holding Back

"You're going to think it's stupid." Alex began haltingly. They were walking back home. They weren't riding their bikes. They knew they'd been gone for days, but their parents would just think they'd been gone for the usual amount of time on a lazy Saturday. It was a hard thing to wrap a head around.

"I don't think you're stupid."

"But"

"Just tell me." Samm protested.

"Well, you know, you're thirteen."

"Uh, yeah."

"And I'm just twelve."

"You'll be thirteen in a few months." Samm reassured.

"But by then, you'll be even older."

"You make it sound like I'm going to be ninety or something – have you been watching Twilight?"

"Ha Ha."

"So what is it then? I'm thirteen. Big deal."

"It IS a big deal. I mean – isn't it? I mean, you're a teenager now. Aren't you going to change?"

Samm blushed in spite of herself. "Change?"

"You know – going to the mall, talking on the phone, dating."

"Dating? Ugh! I'm only thirteen!"

"Well, what about when you turn sixteen and learn to drive before me?"

"You think I won't want to ride bikes anymore? You think I'm just going to drive away and leave you?" Samm's thoughts flashed briefly to the conversation she heard on the Future-shroom. It seemed like a lifetime ago, but Alex was definitely the one leaving HER in that scenario.

"Samm? Where'd you go?" Alex asked.

Samm shook her head. "It's just – you're not making any sense, Alex."

"What if your boyfriend doesn't like me? What if he tells you we can't be friends anymore?"

"Then he'd be an idiot and I'd dump him. We're always going to be best friends, Alex. At least, as far as I'm concerned. Any guy I dated would have to be comfortable with that. Besides, that's still years off. Why are you asking about that?"

"You've just been so…"

"So what? What have I been, Alex?"

"Distant. Since we started looking for A Muse Meant. You've just been distant. Nothing I can put my finger on, exactly."

"I thought we worked all that out in the library that day. Didn't we?"

"Maybe. Not quite though. And maybe it's just me this time, or something I have to get used to."

"Get used to?"

"We are different. Sometimes, each of us are going to go places the other can't."

"But I don't want to go anywhere without you, Alex. You're my best friend!"

"And you're mine. But stop. Don't." Alex took a deep breath and looked Samm square in the face. He was as serious as Samm had ever seen him. "I want you to listen to me carefully Samm. OK?"

"OK." Samm replied meekly.

"OK. Now. Where was I? Oh yeah. Listen. Don't. Don't do it."

"Don't do what, Alex?"

"Don't you dare hold back on my account,
Samantha Cisneros. I'll be with you when I can, and
catch up where I can't, but don't you let anyone, even
me, keep you from being everything you are."

Author Phyl Campbell

Phyl Campbell is Author, Mother, Dreamer —
according to her blog, anyway. She has been writing
since she was old enough to pick up a pencil. This is
her first published book for middle grade readers,
though books for adults and young children are
numerous. And she's still writing.

In 2015, Phyl Campbell also helped a number of
young authors get their stories published. Working
with them inspired her to finish what she started — *A
Muse Meant* being a prime example.

Phyl Campbell has been married for over a decade
and has a son that just turned 13 – though when Phyl
started this book he was 10. He is NOT Alex. And
while he has met the girl Samm is based on, they
didn't attend the same school or spend time together.

Phyl is a picky eater who spends way too much time
playing games and reading articles on Facebook. She
has a great personal library that never has too many
books, but frequently runs out of shelf space.

Questions or comments for Phyl Campbell can be
asked via her webpage www.phylcampbell.com, her
blog www.phylcampbell.blogspot.com, or via the
PhylCampbellAuthorPage on Facebook.

She is phylc_author on Twitter and Instagram.